MASTER OF HANGING CROSS

(An Exmoor Romance: Book 2)

Gail Crane

Published by Aller Books

CONTENTS

Title Page

Copyright

Preface

Chapter 1   1

Chapter 2   14

Chapter 3   32

Chapter 4   51

Chapter 5   68

Chapter 6   87

Chapter 7   106

Chapter 8   124

Chapter 9   145

Chapter 10   162

Chapter 11   181

Chapter 12   195

Thank you   217

About The Author   219

PREFACE

Welcome to the second book in the Exmoor Romance series.

The first book, Flynn's Folly, was set in the village of Larkcombe. This book takes us away from the village and further into the Moor, to the isolated estate of Hanging Cross.

Kate Mackenzie believes she has found her dream job but when she arrives at Hanging Cross and meets its owner, Ethan Cade, she is forced to reconsider.

CHAPTER 1

'Idiot!'

Kate swore as she slammed both feet to the floor and skidded to a halt at the edge of the narrow moorland road, just in time to miss the horse and rider cantering across in front of her.

The ancient Fiesta juddered and stalled and Kate banged her palm against the steering wheel in frustration, her heart hammering against her ribs. Talk about close.

Man and horse had paused a few yards away

It was a magnificent animal. She chuckled to herself. And the horse wasn't bad either.

The man sat easily in the saddle as if he'd been born there, one hand loosely holding the reins while the other rested casually on his thigh. He was tall, at least six feet, probably more. He was bare-headed and Kate caught a glimpse of dark curly hair and a lean, weathered face as he turned his head towards her momentarily.

Mmm. Dishy. Then she revised her opinion as he threw her a withering look and rode on.

Huh. Okay, so maybe she hadn't been quite as

alert as she might have been, she had after all been driving all day, but he could have just made sure she was all right before disappearing.

She stretched the ache from her back and arms. She felt exhausted. For the last hour she had been travelling west along the winding coast road fighting the strengthening on-shore wind that whistled in from the sea below. But she was almost there and she could see the crossroads ahead.

All round her the open moor stretched in purple, mist-shrouded wilderness. To her right it dropped steeply through dense woods towards a rocky cove far below.

Somewhere down there was Hanging Cross.

She took a deep breath. This was so different to the frantic impersonal rush of life in the noisy city she had left behind that morning.

Had she done the right thing in giving up her secure job in London to work on an isolated estate on the Exmoor coast? Perhaps she should have stuck it out, but working with Richard would have been impossible after everything that had happened.

She shrugged. The question was academic. Right or wrong, the choice was made and it was too late to go back now. And working as secretary to one of her favourite novelists in such a beautiful part of the country was going to be heaven compared to being a lowly editorial assistant in a busy city publishing house.

She swivelled the rear-view mirror and looked

at herself. Ugh. She was a mess. Her face was pale, her hair tangled and her clothes creased from long hours driving. She felt tired and grubby, and she looked it. What wouldn't she give to be able to freshen up somewhere before she arrived.

It was hard to believe the interview had been only four weeks ago. Since then she had given in her notice, sold her flat and taken most of her possessions back to her parents' home in Oxfordshire to be stored, and said a final goodbye to her colleagues. Even Richard had seemed to regret her leaving. Too bad. She certainly wasn't going to shed any more tears over him.

In the end, it had been a relief to be leaving the city behind and she had hardly been able to contain her excitement as the day of her journey to Exmoor drew nearer.

There was just one thing that bothered her slightly. One uneasy note that refused to go away.

Those words of Vanessa's kept nudging at her mind and she couldn't help wondering what she had meant by them.

And that look. That first, startled, fleeting look that Vanessa had given her.

§

Vanessa Cade had not been at all how she had pictured her. Certainly not like someone who could afford to stay at Claridges.

Kate had knocked on the door of the penthouse suite feeling slightly nervous, and totally overawed by the luxurious surroundings. This must be the most extravagantly opulent setting imaginable for a job interview.

The door opened and she had her first sight of her prospective employer.

She peered at Kate over a pair of silver-rimmed spectacles which she suddenly whipped off, revealing an expression which Kate could have sworn was one of surprise. But it was gone as soon as it appeared and Kate decided she must have imagined it.

'Miss Cade?'

'And you must be Miss McKenzie?' She smiled and beckoned her in.

Kate guessed she was somewhere in her late sixties though her manner was that of someone much younger. Her long grey-streaked hair was caught up precariously in a large clip on the top of her head and the odd assortment of clothes she was wearing looked as though they might have survived from the Nineteen Twenties and Thirties. In fact, she blended perfectly with the Art Deco room.

She gestured Kate towards the sofa. 'Please, sit down and I'll order some tea. I expect you're famished after your journey.'

'Thank you. That would be lovely. But I haven't really come that far. It's only a short trip on the tube from Clapham.'

Vanessa shuddered. 'How dreadful for you. Can't stand the thing myself. All that shoving and pushing and having your toes trampled on. I always travel by taxi when I'm in London.' She picked up the phone and rang for room service.

Kate sat down and smoothed the skirt of the dark green suit she had put on for the occasion. She knew the plain style suited her petite figure and the green complemented the rich copper colour of her hair and usually she felt good in it, though her preference was for more casual clothes. But Vanessa Cade's flamboyant outfit was making her feel drab by comparison and she wished she had teamed the suit with something a little more colourful than the business-like pale green and white shadow-stripe blouse.

They talked about her work and Kate's reasons for applying for the job. The usual business of interviews.

Then Vanessa said, 'You know, Exmoor, especially where we live, can be very remote. Don't you think you might miss all this? The bright lights and the night life?'

'I suppose I might. But I assume I shall have time off and I can always drive to Taunton or Exeter.'

Vanessa smiled. 'Taunton is hardly London, but I dare say you're right.'

A waiter delivered their tea and Vanessa poured for them both.

'Do have one of those.' She indicated the plate of assorted cakes and helped herself to a large cream puff. 'Can't resist them, I'm afraid,' she said, wiping a smidgeon of cream from her chin.

Kate decided not to tempt fate and settled for an easy-to-eat slice of shortbread.

They sat in silence for a moment, while Vanessa finished her cake and wiped the evidence from her fingers with a linen napkin before speaking.

'I hope you won't be lonely. We do rather rattle around in the place. There's just me and Ethan most of the time. And Ruby, of course. She comes in daily to clean and cook. Then there's the men that work on the estate but they live down in the village.'

'Ethan?'

'My nephew. My brother's son. He owns Hanging Cross. Has done since his parents died some years ago.'

That aroused her curiosity. No mention of a wife. What would he be like, she wondered. Remembering her vow to steer away from relationships for a while, she shrugged the thought away. In any case, judging by Vanessa's age, he was probably at least in his forties if not older. So no danger there.

Then she realised Vanessa was still speaking, almost as though she was talking to herself. 'Although I'm not sure what Ethan will make of …' Her voice trailed off into silence.

Kate was puzzled. 'Make of what?'

Then Vanessa gave herself a shake and smiled broadly. 'Oh, nothing; nothing at all. Take no notice of me. It was just a thought but it's nothing. Now, to business. When can you start?'

§

Kate had forgotten all about it. Had put it down to Vanessa's eccentricity. But now she was actually here in Exmoor and about to arrive at Hanging Cross, the memory was nudging at her again.

She pushed the uneasy thoughts firmly from her mind and reached into the side door pocket of the car for the directions and roughly-drawn mapVanessa had given her. She traced the route with her finger and found the crossroads.

'If this is the right place, there should be a signpost and a marker stone somewhere,' she muttered to herself as she studied the plan.

It would be good to stretch her legs and some fresh air might help to keep her awake.

She laughed. 'And stop me talking to myself.'

She'd walk to the corner.

She opened the door and immediately it was nearly wrenched from its hinges by the fierce moorland wind.

'Ouch!'

Enclosed inside the car, she hadn't realised how rough the weather had become and she had to hang onto the door to prevent it flying from her grasp. The wind whipped her hair sharply round her face, stinging her skin, and she gasped for breath as her lungs were momentarily deprived of air. Fighting against the tug of the wind, she pushed the door shut and leant against the side of the car, breathing hard.

The view was incredible. This was some amazing place she had come to. She had been told that Exmoor was lovely but she hadn't expected anything quite as beautiful as this. She could just imagine Lorna Doone fleeing across this landscape, chased by the evil Carver out to have his wicked way, and being rescued by Jan Ridd. It had been one of her favourite books when she was a teenager full of romantic imaginings and longings. She chuckled to herself. The place was getting to her already.

Again, her hair snapped across her eyes making them water and she fished in the pocket of her jacket to find her hat. Gratefully, she pulled it onto her head, tucking the flying strands of her hair inside and pulling it well down over her ears. The variously coloured bobbles and woolly animals attached to its crown tossed madly in the wind. It had been a mad impulse buy from a stall at a craft fair and she knew she looked silly in it but at least, with her hair securely held back, she could now see where she was going.

She shrugged. 'And who's going to see me up here, anyway?'

Trying to picture the map Vanessa had drawn - she didn't dare to get it out in this wind - she walked towards the crossroads.

A flurry of activity in the sky caught her

attention and she looked up. Overhead a buzzard mewed plaintively as it soared on the wind being mobbed by a small flock of pigeons afraid for the safety of their nests. Two seagulls joined in the attack rending the air with their harsh croaks, and eventually the buzzard, no doubt seeing discretion as the better part of valour, gave up and glided majestically away.

Kate felt a deep sense of solitude. She could almost be the only person in the world. Even at home in the Oxfordshire countryside, she couldn't remember such an atmosphere of peace as she felt here. What Heaven it was.

She found the signpost, an old weathered finger-post indicating a right turn, its faded lettering pointing the way to Hanging Cross. Beneath it stood the marker stone, a meter or so high, surrounded by coarse grass and bracken, and sheltered by a solitary stunted rowan tree. She traced the rough, pitted surface with her fingers, marvelling at the patches of bright-orange and silver lichen that clung to its ancient weathered sides.

She shivered slightly. So this was Hanging Cross.

Vanessa's ancestor, Jacob Cade, had given the name to his house; the house she was now heading for. So romantic, she thought. It was one of the factors in the advert that had attracted her and aroused her curiosity. What kind of place would warrant such a name?

She had put the question to Vanessa at her interview and she recalled her reply as she ran her hand over the stone.

It was built at the end of the eighteenth century, she had told her, by Jacob Cade. He was Ethan's several-times-great grandfather. I've no idea how many greats there are. We did work it out once but I've forgotten. Anyway, he bought several hundred acres of land and built his house on the edge of the moor overlooking the sea. He named it after the gibbet that stood at the nearby crossroads where they used to hang smugglers. All very gruesome if you ask me. Of course, Jacob was a smuggler himself so it's a miracle he didn't end his own life swinging on the gibbet.

Kate glanced at her watch. It was getting late and she needed to move on if she was going to arrive in daylight. After driving most of the day she was desperately in need of rest and the last thing she wanted was to be benighted up here.

She fought her way back to the car. The comfy warmth inside was welcome after the chill of the buffeting wind. She turned the key in the ignition, started the engine and put the car into gear.

Taking the right turn at the crossroads she began to drop down towards the coast. The slopes here were thickly wooded but through the trees she caught occasional glimpses of the sea far below. The road was now little more than a wide track. Grass grew down the centre suggesting it saw little traffic other than that which came and went from the house. It zigzagged downhill in long languorous loops and sharp u-bends. Either side, high clipped hedges, their top branches curving inwards overhead to form a tunnel, gave shelter from the fierce wind but blocked her view of everything apart from the road ahead. So it was something of a surprise when she turned a corner and, without warning, there in front of her stood the house.

Kate blinked. 'Wow. What a place.'

From Vanessa's description she had expected it to be big but this was something else. A sign on the stone boundary wall read 'Hanging Cross' and, underneath, 'Private Property'.

She slowed right down and drove cautiously through the high arched gateway, down the gravelled drive and into a cobbled courtyard, surrounded on three sides by the rambling grey-stone building. Stone-mullioned windows looked out from shady recesses, some facing over the moor, others towards the sea. Heavy timber doors hung on iron hinges within arched timber frames. Creepers covered much of the walls, and an ancient Magnolia climbed almost as far as the small, dusty attic windows in the grey slate roof.

Last night I dreamed I came again to Manderley. The words ran, unbidden, through her head and she had a momentary vision of Mrs Danvers appearing at one of the upper windows pining for her lost Rebecca.

This house was all she had imagined - and

more.

She pulled up alongside a mud-spattered Land Rover parked outside what appeared to be the back door, and switched off the engine. Several pairs of muddy gumboots lay discarded round a heavy sisal door mat. A bowl of water stood to one side.

Ah, dogs, she thought. Good. They had always had dogs at home on the farm but she had not been able to have one in her small London flat and she had missed their company. It would be nice to have them around again.

She yawned involuntarily. The drive from London had taken much longer than she'd expected. Perhaps she shouldn't have tried to do the whole journey in one day but splitting it would have entailed an over-night stay somewhere and the cost of fuel for the car had already eaten into her meagre savings.

She leant back in the seat and stretched, trying to ease the aching muscles of her back and neck.

Where was everyone? It was strange that nobody had come out to meet her. The car tyres had made enough noise on the gravel to alert anyone in the house.

She rubbed her eyes and yawned again. Well, she wanted a change from city life, some peace and quiet, some of that vanishing tranquillity people seemed to be always seeking but rarely finding, and it looked very much as though she was going to find it here. She supposed she should go and knock on a door but she'd just sit here for a second or two longer. Her eyes felt so heavy it wouldn't hurt to close them a while....

... She woke with a start. The sound of voices insinuated itself into her dreams, dragging her back to reality. She sat up and pushed back her hat, which had slipped forward over her face covering her eyes and nose, and turned in the direction of the voices.

She swallowed.

Her mouth went dry and a frisson of excitement rippled down her back.

Walking towards her was the most wickedly attractive man she had ever seen. There didn't seem to be an inch of spare fat on him. He looked all lean, hard, muscle. She saw a tanned, chiselled face under a mass of thick, curling dark hair and realised with a jolt that it was him. The rider she had seen on the road. It must be. He was dressed for riding in knee-length brown leather boots over black breeches moulded to muscular thighs, and a well-worn hip-length, sleeveless leather jacket over a brown and cream check shirt with sleeves rolled up to his elbows revealing deeply-tanned arms. Just how sexy could you get? Everything about him said 'male' with a capital M.

Kate blinked.

God, she thought. I'm in love.

So much for her resolution to forget about men. This one just oozed sex-appeal.

CHAPTER 2

'**G**ood God!'

Ethan Cade stared at the battered Fiesta parked in his yard. There was no mistaking it. Painted flowers in clashing colours rambled chaotically over its rust-pocked body and orange baler twine held down the tailgate. It was at least twenty years old and looked it and the last time he had seen it, it had been heading straight for him.

He handed his horse over to the young stable lad who stood waiting, and walked across to investigate.

What on earth was she wearing on her head? The hat reminded him of his grandmother's multi-coloured knitted tea-cosy, only this had an odd assortment of bobbles and woolly animals hanging from its crown. The girl looked as unconventional as her car.

She turned towards him, rubbing her eyes as though she'd just woken up. As he looked at her through the car window, a vague ripple of un-ease shivered through him. He pushed it away and bent down to open the door for her.

He had a brief impression of green eyes in a pale face, then a pair of trim, jeans-clad legs as she swung round and climbed out of the car. She stood, her eyes about level with his chin, smiling at him. It was only when a slight flush pinked her cheeks and she whipped off the hat as if embarrassed to be caught wearing it, that he realised he had been staring.

And continued to stare, as he watched the thick copper-coloured hair tumble round her shoulders.

Surely this couldn't be his aunt's new assistant?

But it was. He just knew it. The sinking feeling in the pit of his stomach told him without a doubt that it was. No wonder Vanessa had been so cagey about her when he'd asked what she was like.

He had lived with his aunt long enough not to be surprised by anything she did. At least, he thought he had. She had always been scatty, as far back as he could remember, but it seemed the older she got, the more eccentric she became, and this was reaching new levels, even for her.

He grimaced. He would tackle his aunt later.

He took a deep breath and pasted on what he hoped was a welcoming smile. This was not going to be easy.

'I'm so sorry,' she was saying. 'I must have dropped off.'

'Don't apologise. I know how tiring it can

be driving from London. I take it you are Miss McKenzie?'

'Yes, but please call me Kate.'

She held out her hand and he took it in his.

'I'm Ethan Cade.'

'You're Ethan Cade?'

'Last time I looked, yes. You seem surprised?'

'I um … expected you to be,' she swallowed, 'older.'

'Older?'

He saw a faint blush warm her cheeks.

'Sorry, I didn't mean to be rude. It's just that when Miss Cade said she had a nephew, I pictured him as being, well…'

His mouth twisted in a wry half-smile as he supplied the word for her. 'Older.'

She seemed to be searching for something to say and finding nothing to fit the bill. He decided to help her out.

'It's okay. My aunt is considerably older than my father. Hence the difference in our ages.'

'Ah, I see.' Then, with an abrupt change of subject, she gestured towards the house.

'This is amazing. It's even more beautiful than I imagined.'

A glow of pleasure licked through him. He loved Hanging Cross. Had given half his life to restoring it from the ravages of his father's neglect.

'Yes,' he agreed. 'It is beautiful, isn't it. It has an interesting history, too.'

'Really? I'd love to hear about it some time.'

'I expect my aunt will tell you plenty about it in due course,' he said. 'You will discover, if you haven't already, that there is nothing my aunt enjoys more than a good gossip. Now, I expect you're anxious to get settled in and, as my aunt appears to have taken herself off for a walk, I suggest we take your bags and go and find Ruby.'

'They're in the back.'

He watched as Kate untied the baler-twine and lifted the back of the Fiesta.

He couldn't resist asking. 'Did you really drive that all the way from London?'

'I know.' She laughed. 'It is a bit in-your-face, isn't it? But you have to admit it's different.'

'It's certainly that.'

'And much more reliable than it looks.' She grinned. 'Actually, I think it's had so many new parts it's almost a new car by now.'

Somehow he doubted that. 'Well, at least the brakes appear to work, for which I and my horse must be thankful.'

She grimaced. 'Oh, dear. Yes, I'm sorry about that. But you must admit, you did rather ride out in front of me.'

'If you are going to live here, you will have to get used to it. Animals on the road are a constant hazard.'

'I'll try and remember.'

Was that a note of sarcasm in her voice? He leaned over and took her suitcase from the boot, leaving her to bring the small holdall, and led the way across the yard towards the house, adapting his long stride to her shorter one.

'I didn't really need a car when I was in London you see,' she explained as they walked. 'So Vicky, my flat mate, and I used to borrow this one from the girl downstairs. She was a bit flower-power - or she would have been if she'd been born twenty years earlier. Anyway, it was cheap - very cheap actually - so I bought it. Life on a shoestring and all that.'

His hands clenched. Money. Why did she have to go and mention money?

He noticed her look at him and knew his feelings must be reflected in his face. He shook his head. This whole situation was positively spooky. In fact, right now, more than anything else, he needed to be alone so he could re-assure himself that he wasn't dreaming it all.

The sooner he handed Miss McKenzie over to Vanessa, the better he would feel. And from now on, he would just have to keep his distance. That way, maybe he could cope; at least until he had spoken to his aunt.

One thing was for sure. She would have to find a new secretary because there was no way he was going to have this one living under the same roof as him.

They reached the back door of the house and he pushed it open with his heel and held it for her to go through.

§

Kate was perplexed by Ethan's sudden change of mood.

She had sensed a hint of something being not quite right ever since he had come to greet her. One minute he was friendly, the next he seemed to back off. She shook herself. She was tired, and was probably imagining it.

She walked past him into the biggest kitchen she had ever seen. A huge scrubbed oak table stood in the centre of the room, one end of its surface piled with papers, books, crockery and various cooking utensils. Rugs, some of which had clearly seen better days, covered parts of the flag-stoned floor in front of what had once been a large open fireplace but was now occupied by a modern Aga.

She had time for only a fleeting impression of clutter and chaos before it seemed all hell was let loose. Two dogs, a spaniel and a labrador, bounded into the room, almost knocking her over, as they threw themselves at Ethan Cade's feet, tails wagging and tongues lolling in an ecstasy of adoration and joy.

Well, at least somebody loves him, she thought.

Ethan gave them both a cursory stroke then pointed to the baskets in front of the Aga.

'Bed,' he told them. They obeyed immediately.

'They're gorgeous,' Kate said. 'What are they called?'

'The spaniel is Belle and the labrador is Otto.'

'I love dogs but I couldn't really have pets in London. Not in a third floor flat anyway.'

'These aren't pets, they're working dogs. They do as they're told.'

I bet everyone else does, too, Kate thought. She was rapidly revising her initial impression of him and guessed this was a man used to having his orders obeyed. By people as well as dogs. Thank goodness she was working for his aunt and not for him. He was altogether too unsettling.

He dropped her case on the floor before crossing to another door and calling, 'Ruby!' Then he pointed vaguely towards a chair and told her, 'You can wait here. Ruby will show you to your room.'

Then, to her surprise, he turned and went back outside leaving her alone. She put the holdall down next to the suitcase and her laid her jacket on the chair with her handbag.

'Well, what happens now, I wonder?' she asked the dogs.

They thumped their tails at the sound of her voice and she bent down and stroked them, enjoying the feel of their warm bodies and silky coats. They wriggled with pleasure and rolled onto their backs, offering their soft bellies for tickling.

'It's a good job 'He' can't see us now,' she told them with a grin. 'He would probably send me to my bed as well.'

The dogs wagged their agreement.

A sudden voice made her start.

'Miss McKenzie?'

Kate jumped up and turned.

The woman standing in the doorway was short and plump with greying brown hair plaited over her ears and the two plaits taken up and somehow fixed together on the top of her head. Kate guessed she was probably in her late forties though it was difficult to tell as her hair style and clothing gave the appearance of someone much older. Her hands were thrust into the pocket of a flowery, old-fashioned pinafore-style apron.

Kate smiled at her. 'Oh, hello. I didn't hear you come in. Are you Ruby?'

She very much hoped she was because she really needed to find her room before she went to sleep again. Also, she needed a wash as, on top of everything else, her hands were now liberally coated with dog dust.

The woman nodded. Kate was uncomfortably aware that Ruby was studying her closely, She hadn't looked in a mirror for a while. Perhaps she had a smut on her nose or her mascara had run or something.

Ruby shook her head slowly from side to side.

'My,' she said, 'the master's going to love you.'

Kate blinked. 'The master?' Was she talking about Ethan Cade? Certainly that title would suit him. 'If you mean Mr Cade, we've already met.'

'Ah, so you'll know, then.'

Kate was about to reply when the back door

opened and the dogs flew joyously across the room to be greeted by Vanessa Cade.

Kate looked with affectionate amusement at her new employer. She was clothed in her usual odd selection of period costume, her one concession to modernity being a man's grey herringbone overcoat that hung almost to her ankles and flapped open as she walked, to reveal a silky, vividly-coloured floral dress with a drooping handkerchief hemline. She swept the cloche hat from her head and dropped it on top of the clutter on the kitchen table.

'Hello, my lovelies,' she cried, bending down and throwing her arms round the dogs' necks while they panted adoringly in her face.

'That's enough now.' Vanessa gave them both a final pat and stood up. 'Off to your beds. There's good dogs.'

Reluctantly they trotted back to their baskets.

Vanessa placed her hands in the small of her back and stretched. Strands of her grey hair had been pulled from their clips and now fell across her face. She pushed them back, carelessly, and smiled at Kate.

'Hello, my dear. I see you two have met.' She turned to Ruby. 'I can look after Kate, now, Ruby. I expect you have plenty to do.'

Ruby nodded. 'Always something needs doing.' She spoke to Kate. 'Will you be coming down to dinner, Miss? Or would you like something quietly in your room after your journey?'

'Oh, that's kind of you to offer, but I think I would rather eat down here. And, please, do call me Kate.'

Ruby huffed slightly. 'I don't know about that, I'm sure.'

'But 'Miss' is so formal, don't you think?'

'Well, we'll see. I'll lay you a place at dinner then.'

Kate gave up. 'Thank you. That will be lovely.'

Vanessa divested herself of gloves and scarf and dropped them alongside her discarded hat with the rest of the clutter on the table. She caught Ruby's glance as the woman left the room, and pulled a face at Kate. 'Oh, dear. I'm afraid the chaos you see is mine. Ruby disapproves terribly and so does Ethan. He's such a well organised person but I do find excessive tidiness so stifling. Don't you agree?'

Kate was saved from having to think of an answer as Vanessa ploughed on without waiting. 'Did you have a good journey? You must be exhausted after driving all that way. Let's get you to your room. I'm sure you must be dying to wash and change. Let me take that holdall for you.'

With relief, Kate picked up the rest of her things and followed Vanessa through another door opposite the one through which she had entered with Ethan, into a square hall which was obviously the main entrance to the house. Opposite a huge oak front door, a wide staircase led up to the next floor.

The walls of the hall and staircase were hung with portraits. In several of them she could see more than a slight resemblance to Vanessa and Ethan.

'They're mostly family,' said Vanessa, confirming her thoughts. Pausing half way up the flight, she pointed to a cracked painting of a round-faced, be-wigged man dressed for riding, standing next to his horse and dogs. 'That old reprobate is Jacob.'

'The one who built the house?'

'That's the one. With ill-gotten gains from smuggling,' she added with relish.

'He's rather handsome isn't he?' Like Ethan, Kate added to herself.

Vanessa studied him for a moment, head on one side.

'I suppose he is. Piratical, don't you think?'

'Mm, I can just imagine him as a smuggler dragging in the contraband by lantern light with a storm raging and the sea crashing onto the rocks.'

'What a romantic you are.'

'I suppose I am. But so must you be. You couldn't write such wonderful books if you weren't.'

'You're right, I am. Living in this house helps, of course. It's just brimming with atmosphere and romance.'

She moved on up the stairs.

'These two,' Vanessa stopped in front of a pair of portraits hanging side by side, 'are my brother,

Charles, and his wife. Ethan's parents.'

'Goodness, the likeness is incredible. There's no doubting they are father and son. Do they live near here?'

Vanessa shook her head. 'They're dead. Charles drove them both over the cliff almost fifteen years ago,'

'You mean …?'

'No, no. Not suicide. It was an accident.

'How awful.' Maybe that accounted for Ethan's strange personality. Loosing both parents like that must have been a terrible experience for a young boy.

'I suppose it was.' Vanessa shrugged. 'Best thing that could've happened for Hanging Cross, though.'

'Oh?'

'It gave Ethan a chance to rescue it before it reached the point of no return. I'm afraid my brother had more love for drink than he did for Hanging Cross. The whole place was going to pot until Ethan took over.'

How old would Ethan have been then? Kate wondered. Barely out of his teens, probably. And not only had he lost both parents but he'd had to take on the responsibility of the estate as well. That must have been some challenge for a young man that age and must have taken a great deal of commitment and hard work. Which maybe accounted for his strange manner.

They reached the top of the stairs and Vanessa

led her along a corridor and into a room at the far end.

With an expansive wave of her arm, she said, 'This is yours. I do hope you will like it. I thought you might enjoy having a view of the sea.'

Kate was captivated. 'It's beautiful,' she said.

The room was far larger than any bedroom she had slept in before. It was furnished with an oak-framed double bed and a large oak wardrobe with a matching chest of drawers next to it. Opposite the door was the most enormous square bay window with a chest seat beneath it, scattered with tapestry cushions which matched the heavy curtains and, opposite the bed, a blue and cream tiled fireplace was laid with logs.

'A real fire?' she exclaimed. 'In a bedroom? What luxury.'

'Not such a luxury come winter, I can assure you. You'll be glad of it then.'

'In that case, I shall look forward to winter so that I can enjoy it.'

Vanessa laughed. 'It'll be here soon enough, don't you worry. Now, through there is your bathroom.' She indicated a door between the fireplace and the window. 'I shall leave you to get settled. Come down when you're ready.'

Kate was thrilled with the room. It was far grander than she had expected. She decided to unpack later. What she really wanted right now was to have a shower and get into clean clothes.

She opened her case and took out some clean

underwear. She wondered what she should wear for dinner and decided on a heavy cotton skirt and a lambs-wool sweater. As she pulled them out of the case a photograph slipped out with them and slid onto the bed.

She picked it up and grimaced at the handsome face that grinned back at her from the print.

'Huh, I thought I'd seen the last of you,' she muttered.

Richard was part of the reason she had come here to Exmoor, as far away as she could from the big city and the shallow, materialistic people she'd been working with. The last thing she wanted now was this reminder of the man she had been in love with and who, she had thought, had loved her, too.

Across the back, in his flamboyant scrawl, he had written, To Kate. All my love, Richard.

She sat looking at it for a second or two, as her memory took her reluctantly back to the heady days before she had found him out.

She could hear him now protesting, 'It's not what you're thinking, Kate'. But, of course, it had been exactly what she'd been thinking. How naïve she had been. She'd learned her lesson the hard way and her consequent growing-up had been sudden and painful.

It would be a while before she fell into that trap again.

That was another attraction of this job. Tucked away quietly in a backwater, working for a woman novelist, would be a pleasant change from bright lights and parties.

How the photo had got into her case was a mystery. She must have picked it up without realising when she cleared her belongings from the flat. Everything else to do with him she had burned or thrown away the night she had discovered him with the girl from the admin department.

She shrugged and grasped the photo in both hands. 'You know where you can go, don't you.' She tore it in two and dropped it into the wastepaper basket that stood next to the fireplace.

So much for Richard. In future, she would make very certain of her man before giving him her heart. She banished thoughts of him firmly from her mind. He was the past - and she meant to keep him there.

She stripped off her travel-weary clothes, slipped into her robe, found her bag of toiletries and went to investigate the bathroom.

It was sheer luxury compared with the one she had shared in her Clapham flat and she revelled in the pleasure of showering in water that was actually hot. What bliss. Feeling relaxed and clean at last, she wrapped herself in one of the soft bath towels that had been provided for her and went back into the bedroom.

She stopped at the window and knelt on the window seat, resting her elbows on the ledge. The view from here was incredible. She could see across a wide expanse of sloping lawn, dotted with apple and pear trees, to the edge of the cliff and the sea far below. Oak and birch trees, and others she couldn't see well enough to identify, covered the hill slopes to one side of the lawn behind the house, trailing off into scrub and bracken. A suggestion of a path led downwards through the bracken; not a proper path, just trampled grass; as though there had been a path there once but it had since fallen out of use. Intriguing. She wondered if it went anywhere.

She turned her head and could just see the corner of a terrace that presumably ran along the other side of the house. A movement caught her eye as a figure stepped into view.

It was Ethan Cade, his tall frame outlined against the glow of the late afternoon sun as he stood with his back to her, hands thrust deep into his trouser pockets, looking out towards the sea.

§

Ethan stopped at the end of the terrace along which he had been pacing back and forth for some time, deep in thought. Shading his eyes from the sun's glare, he gazed across the long sweep of lawn in front of him, towards the vastness of the sea beyond. Behind the house, the wooded slopes climbed steeply up to the open moor, the trees beginning to cast their shadows across the grass.

He drew a deep, satisfied breath, relishing the sharp coldness of the clean Exmoor air as it pierced his lungs. His family had lived here since Jacob built the house in the early eighteenth century and Ethan loved every inch of the place.

How different things might have been, though, had his father, after a long evening at the Ship Inn, not misjudged a sharp bend and driven both himself and Ethan's mother over the edge of the cliff. It had taken many years and a lot of hard work to restore the fortune his father had frittered away on fast cars and women. During that time, Ethan had built himself a property empire, and slowly and painfully brought Hanging Cross back to its former glory.

All in all, life was good.

Or it might have been if it wasn't for Caroline.

At the thought of her, his dark eyes clouded with anger. The sooner that little matter was dealt with, the better. Perhaps then, his life could return to normal and he could begin to live for the future without being haunted by the past.

Except that, now, there was this new secretary of his aunt's - and quite how he was going to deal with her, he hadn't the faintest idea. One thing was certain though, deal with her he must.

He turned as Vanessa came along the terrace towards him

Perhaps now he would find out what on earth she thought she was doing employing Kate McKenzie. He opened his mouth to speak but she put up her hand and jumped in before he could say anything.

'Ethan, I know what you're going to say.'

'What were you thinking of, Nessa? You must have known?'

CHAPTER 3

From her seat at the window, Kate could hear their voices clearly. She was torn between not wanting to eavesdrop and curiosity about what they were saying. She knew she should move away but the temptation to listen was irresistible.

Vanessa's reply was too faint to hear but Ethan's next words were clear enough. 'You've put me in an impossible position. You do know that, don't you? And what about Ruby?'

'It's all right. I've taken care of that.'

Kate could feel her nerves fizzing as her heart beat uncomfortably in her throat. She was pretty certain they were discussing her. She guessed by the fading of their voices that they were moving away. She was glad. She didn't want to hear any more.

A muffled ring-tone broke the silence. She found her bag and pulled out her mobile. As the name and number appeared on the screen, she felt her pulse quicken uncomfortably.

Richard. Damn it. Just what she didn't need.

She hesitated, her finger hovering. Then she punched the button and cancelled the call.

She thought she had made it perfectly clear that she was finished with him. The cheek of the man. Surely he wasn't going to try and resurrect their relationship after the way he had behaved.

She shivered. Sitting in nothing but a towel, she was beginning to feel cold and it was time she got dressed for dinner. Richard's call had unsettled her and perhaps some company would help put him from her mind.

But the atmosphere at dinner did nothing to improve Kate's mood.

The meal was excellent. Ruby was clearly a talented cook and the food was delicious. Kate could see she was going to have to watch her weight and make sure she balanced hours of desk work with plenty of exercise. She was sure there would be lots of opportunity for long walks through the woods and over the moor and she was looking forward to exploring the area.

Ruby was an odd character. She could have been a servant in a Victorian novel the way she jealously guarded her duties and persisted in calling Ethan 'Master'. She didn't eat with them but just served up the meal and disappeared to eat her own in the kitchen.

The conversation was mainly between herself and Vanessa, who was her usual charming self. But Ethan, though determinedly polite, made no attempt to join in and it was obvious that things between him and his aunt were strained.

Kate was glad when the meal was over and she was able to plead tiredness and escape to her room. Despite the awkwardness of the evening and the strange surroundings, she fell asleep almost as soon as her head hit the pillow.

§

....She was on a swing; a child's swing; gliding backwards and forwards; the wind soughing in her ears as she moved. Something was pulling her upwards; it was tight round her neck and she couldn't breathe. Then the swing was gone and she was hanging from the gibbet; swaying back and forth in the wind, high above the moor. She couldn't see. She was blind. No - a blindfold was tied round her eyes. People were laughing at her; shouting and jeering, and someone had picked up a stick and was hitting the gibbet post, knocking, knocking. Then strong arms grabbed her, lifted her down, and she was on the saddle in front of her rescuer. She relaxed against him as he gently removed her blindfold and she looked up into the face of ...

Ethan Cade. She woke with a start, struggling to extricate herself from the duvet which had somehow become twisted round her.

Sun streamed through the window and the sound of men's voices drifted up to her from the garden. She looked at her clock. 'Oh ...damn!' It couldn't be that time, surely? She couldn't believe she'd overslept on her first morning.

She leapt out of bed and pulled back the curtains. Two men were busy ramming in a fence post. Well that explained the knocking sound that had woken her from her dream. But why on earth had she been dreaming about Ethan Cade? She was beginning to think that she didn't even like him, let alone see him in the role of a rescuing hero.

No time to think of him now, though. She had to get a move on.

If only she had finished unpacking last night. She rummaged in her case for something presentable and un-creased and settled on a pair of trousers and a crinkle cotton shirt. She had the fastest shower of her life - hair washing would have to wait until tomorrow - threw on her clothes and rushed downstairs.

Ruby was clearing the table when she arrived, breathless, in the kitchen.

'I'm so sorry I'm late, Ruby,' she apologised. 'I suppose everyone else has eaten?'

'Master always has breakfast early then goes riding before he starts work,' Ruby informed her as she presented Kate with a rack of toast and a pot of coffee. 'Cereal's on the side there if you want it. Or would you prefer something cooked?'

'Thank you but this will be fine. I couldn't possibly manage cooked after that wonderful meal last night.'

She was sure that Ruby almost smiled.

She spread honey on a slice of toast and poured

some coffee into a mug. 'Do you know where can I find Vanessa?'

'I expect Miss Vanessa will be in her writing room. Down the end of the hall. Last room on the left.'

Kate finished eating in record time and knocked on Vanessa's door just a few minutes after nine.

Vanessa called her in. She was sitting at an old-fashioned dark-oak bureau, which stood under one of two large windows, reading a letter. The room appeared quite small but maybe that was because it was so full of furniture and clutter. Two walls were covered from floor to ceiling with shelves filled to overflowing with assorted books. A chintz-covered sofa and easy chair were drawn up in front of a log fire and the centre of the room was taken up with a long dark-oak refectory table covered with papers and books. Under the second window stood a smaller desk covered with papers and assorted items of stationery.

Kate wondered where she would be working. Every available surface was covered with clutter and there didn't seem to be any spare space.

Vanessa looked up from her letter and smiled. 'Goodness, you are an early bird. You should have had a bit of a lie in after all that travelling yesterday.'

Kate grimaced inwardly. If only she'd known. She could just have done with an extra hour in bed.

'Never mind,' Vanessa continued. 'Come on in.

Now, I thought we'd spend the morning getting you settled. There won't be much for you to do this morning anyway. I can't remember whether I mentioned it at your interview, but I prefer to be alone when I'm writing so I usually dictate everything into one of those machines then hand it over to be typed up. Will that suit you?'

'That's fine. I'm used to using a dictating machine.'

'Ah, good. The trouble is,' she looked vaguely round the room, 'I'm not sure what I've done with it. I have a feeling I left it with Helen. She's been doing a bit of typing for me while I've been without help. I suppose you wouldn't be kind enough to go and ask her for me, would you?

'Helen?'

'Ethan's secretary. But first let me show you your room. Your office is next to mine.'

Kate followed her into a room similar in size to the one they had just left but much more spartan. A large desk stood under the window with a surprisingly modern computer and printer. An old brown wing chair stood to one side of the fireplace in which a log fire had been laid ready for lighting. Along one wall was arranged a filing cabinet, a small empty bookcase and some shelves stacked with stationery and various computer bits.

Vanessa waved an arm to encompass the room. 'I'm afraid it's a bit bare at the moment but do feel free to do whatever you like to cheer it up. I do think a room needs a bit of clutter to feel really comfortable. Don't you?'

'Um, yes. Thank you.'

'I expect you know how to drive that contraption?' She grimaced at the computer. 'I did try once but I swear it has a mind of its own. Always seemed to do what *it* wanted to do rather than what *I* wanted, so I gave up.'

Kate chuckled. 'I know what you mean. But, yes, I'll be fine. No problem.'

'Good. Now, if I point you in the right direction, perhaps you could go and find Helen for me?' She moved back into the passage. 'She'll be in the estate office. Go back past the kitchen then keep going and you'll find it right at the end, next to the garden door.'

Kate retraced her steps back to the kitchen and carried on, past several other doors until she reached the last one. This must be it. It would be so easy to get lost in this house with its rambling corridors but no doubt she would get used to it eventually.

She knocked on the door.

There was no response.

She knocked again, harder, then jumped as a man's voice roared out.

'Don't just stand there. Come in.'

Oh-oh. The voice was horribly familiar - and definitely not Helen. Had she come to the wrong room?

It was not a promising start to the day.

She straightened her back, lifted her chin and

pushed open the door. Opposite her, Ethan was sitting in a black leather swivel chair, behind a huge oak, leather-topped desk, talking on the phone, and he did not look happy. Brusquely, he told the caller to hold, clamped his hand over the mouthpiece and rocked forward in the chair, eyebrows raised in question.

'Yes?' he snapped.

No. Definitely not happy.

Kate found herself inexplicably tongue-tied. Sitting behind that great desk, his six-foot plus frame filling the chair, the man exuded power and confidence and … yes, she had to admit … sex-appeal by the bucket-load.

'Um,' she stuttered, 'er, I'm sorry. You're busy …'

'How observant of you. Shouldn't you also be busy? With my aunt?'

Kate felt her face grow hot. Really. Sex-appeal he might have, but did he have to be quite so rude? She squared her shoulders. 'Actually, I was looking for Helen. Vanessa wondered if she had left her dictating machine here.'

Both hands still clasped round the phone, he pointed impatiently across the room. 'If she has, it'll be in there somewhere. Help yourself.'

Glad to be able to hide her burning face, Kate turned to the cupboard he had indicated.

Ethan resumed his phone conversation. 'Sorry to keep you waiting. How long do you think it will take? …. How long? … Okay … No - no. Not your fault. It can't be helped. I'll contact the agency. … I'm sure they will. Don't worry. … Yes, I'll let you know …'

All Kate could find was an ancient Dictaphone. Surely this couldn't be what she was looking for? But then, knowing Vanessa, she could imagine that this was exactly the kind of machine she might be using. She held it up towards Ethan, raising her eyebrows in silent query. He nodded. She collected up the power leads and microphone that went with it and mouthed a thank you as she opened the door to leave the room.

If anything, his expression was darker than ever. She guessed it was not proving to be a satisfactory conversation.

§

Ethan returned the phone to its stand and sighed with frustration. God knew how he was going to manage without his secretary. He supposed he could arrange for a girl to come out from the London office but it would mean someone else having to double up. No, better that he try the temp agency first.

And as if that wasn't enough to cope with, there was still Kate McKenzie to deal with as well. He watched the door close behind her and wondered what the hell he was going to do. He was painfully aware that he had been rude to the girl. Unforgivably so. After all, it was hardly her fault.

The fault was his aunt's for bringing the girl

here in the first place. He couldn't understand why on earth she had done it and when he'd tackled her about it, she had mumbled some sort of excuse that hadn't made any sense at all. But she must, surely, have been aware of the consequences?

She could be incredibly stubborn when it suited her and when he'd told her that her new secretary would have to go, she had dug her heels in and resolutely refused to even think about replacing her. So now he was mad with his aunt and mad with the girl. But, most of all, he was mad with himself for minding so much. For letting it get to him the way it had.

He rested his elbows on the desk and cradled his head in his hands. He could hardly believe the effect Miss McKenzie was having on him. How hard he was having to fight to control his reactions.

The day she'd arrived and whipped off that ridiculous hat, it had hit him like a punch in the guts. All the memories he had been trying so hard to shut out for the past year came flooding back. His body had responded immediately and he'd felt the same old adrenalin rush, the same pounding in his veins, that he'd felt when he and Caroline Carpenter had first met.

Memories of that evening flooded back; the evening of the Carpenters' dance. He hadn't wanted to go. They were Vanessa's friends, not his, and dancing was definitely not one of his preferred pastimes, but Vanessa had bullied him into taking her. He had spent the early part of the evening playing poker with some of the other men and, to his surprise, was enjoying the evening - until Vanessa had asked him to escort her to the buffet table.

Even now, the memory still cut deep.

He'd heard that the Carpenters' daughter was home from an extended holiday abroad. There had even been rumours that she had grown into something of a beauty. But nothing had prepared him for the real thing.

As she turned towards him, silky hair rippling round her face and shoulders, and looked at him with those deep green eyes, he'd felt his stomach flip.

She'd smiled at him; that sensual, provocative smile that she did so well; and, with a voice like honey, she'd said, 'Hi, there,' and he had known, even then, that he wanted to marry her. And he had. Six months later, in an extravagantly grand wedding that hit all the society columns, they had vowed to love, honour etc.

He choked back a sound that was part laugh, part sob. Well, the bit about forsaking all others hadn't lasted long. Barely a month, in fact. The length of their honeymoon cruise.

My God, he thought, how could I have been so blind? Two days back from their honeymoon and she was in someone else's bed. She hadn't contested the divorce. As soon as she knew she would get a hefty financial settlement, she had disappeared with her lover, leaving her solicitor to finalise matters.

It had been such bitter humiliation to realise that she had only married him for his money. Marry in haste and repent at leisure. Well, he had no intention of repenting at leisure. The sooner this divorce was through the better, then perhaps he could get on with his life.

One thing was for certain; he wasn't going to go down that road again. Once was enough and Miss Kate McKenzie was much too disturbing for comfort. Definitely no-go territory. The moment she had made her comment about life on a shoestring, he'd felt the adrenalin shot, warning him not to fall for it again.

This time he would listen to his head not his hormones. And if his body tried to persuade him otherwise, he would just have to keep his distance and cultivate a fancy for cold showers.

The trouble was, he was well aware that he was behaving badly towards her. It was totally out of character for him and totally unfair on her. She had done nothing wrong and he knew he was making her pay for his own problems.

He must make an effort to be nice to her. Avoid her as much as possible but be pleasant and polite when they had to meet.

And now, to cap it all, somehow he had to manage without Helen.

He turned to the file lying open on the desk. He had promised his estate manager, Harry

Crawford, he would get the information on the field boundary to him this afternoon and the way the day had gone so far, it looked as though he was going to have to deal with it himself.

Old estate plans were kept in the library together with deeds and papers going back to Jacob's time. They had always fascinated him and, if he had more time, this was a task he would have enjoyed. As it was, time was in short supply.

He looked at his watch. Library first. Then, after lunch, he would ring the agency.

Damn. Why did Helen have to go and break her wrist!

§

Kate made her way along the rambling passageways back to Vanessa's writing room. The more she saw of the house, the more she longed to be able to explore it. As it had been built by a smuggler, perhaps it had secret passages, or even tunnels leading down to the coast. The romantic in her was intrigued and she determined to ask Vanessa if she could look around.

'Of course,' Vanessa told her. 'Though I'm not sure you will find any secret tunnels. If there ever were any, I imagine they have long since been blocked up. Although there have been stories. When we were children, Charles and I used to play in the old chapel and pretend we were smugglers.'

'What fun. I haven't noticed a chapel. Where is it?'

But Vanessa shrugged and shook her head dismissively. 'Oh, it's not used now. Abandoned.'

Kate had a distinct impression that Vanessa regretted mentioning it, especially as she then instantly changed the subject.

Now,' she said, 'if you will just get me set up with this contraption, I shall spend the morning dictating. Then you will have something to type up after lunch. Meanwhile, why don't you go and browse in the library? If you are interested in the house, you'll find a whole shelf of information on its history over the years. Who knows? You may even discover a tunnel or two.'

Kate worked out how to fit a fresh tape into the machine and plugged it in to the wall socket. 'You know you can get digital dictating machines now?' she said as she connected the microphone.

'You mean like computers?' Vanessa shook her head. 'No thanks. This does what I tell it to.'

Well it would be a novelty, Kate thought. She hadn't even seen one of these before let alone used one.

She made sure Vanessa had everything she needed for her work and then made her way towards the library.

Perhaps, among the books, there would be something about the chapel Vanessa had mentioned. And that was another puzzle. Why had she changed the subject so obviously? Just what was going on in this house? There were so many undercurrents. Looks exchanged.

Comments made and withdrawn.

Then there was Ethan.

She really didn't know what to make of Ethan Cade. She couldn't deny she was attracted to him physically. What girl wouldn't be? With his tall, muscular body, that thick, dark hair and those deep brown eyes, he was more drop-dead gorgeous than any man had a right to be. She shivered at the thought.

But personality-wise he was something else.

Most of the time he gave every impression of disliking her intensely. He was barely polite to her. And yet, when they first met, he had been friendly and charming - for about five minutes. What had happened to make him change? However much she thought about it, she couldn't think of any reason at all.

She reached the library and pushed open the heavy oak door. The lights were on and a pile of papers covered the large central table.

She was not alone.

Ethan Cade looked up from the document he was reading and she found herself looking into those same sexy brown eyes she had been thinking about only a moment ago.

Oops, she thought. Bad timing. Perhaps some other time.

'Sorry,' she said, beginning to back out of the room. 'I didn't realise anyone was in here.'

Then he confounded her completely by smiling.

'That's all right. Come in.'

What had happened to the bad-tempered man he had been earlier? He now seemed to be the same friendly person he had been when she first arrived.

'Thanks.' She closed the door behind her. 'Are you sure I'm not disturbing you?'

'No. I'm just looking for some papers.' He gave a wry grin. ' I think I owe you an apology for this morning. I'm not usually quite so bad tempered but I'd just been told that my secretary has managed to break her wrist. So I'm having to do my own admin work.' He indicated the papers on the table. 'Not something I'm used to.'

I'll bet, thought Kate. No wonder he had been in a bad mood. 'Apology accepted. But how will you manage? It sounds as though she'll be off work for some time.'

'Yes, it looks like it.'

'Can't you get a temp?'

'I hope so. I'll be ringing the agency later when I've sorted this lot out. Anyway, that's my problem. What brings you to the library? Was there something you wanted?'

'Nothing specific. Vanessa said I could come and browse. She doesn't need me till this afternoon and I was hoping to find some background information about the house and its history.'

'You're interested?' His expression softened and Kate noticed again how his eyes lit up with pleasure when she showed curiosity about the house.

'I think it's fascinating. Vanessa has told me a bit about Jacob Cade and his connection with smuggling. And the house has such atmosphere.' She gestured round the room. 'You can almost see men in cut-away coats and knee-breeches hurrying to hide the contraband before the excise man arrives.'

Ethan laughed and she had a tantalising glimpse of the real man that might be lurking behind that chilly exterior.

'Vanessa used to tell me stories,' he said, 'of how, when she and my father were children, they would dress up in clothes from the attic and pretend to be eighteenth century gentry.'

'Muslin dresses and powdered wigs I suppose?'

'Not quite, though I believe there was once an unfortunate episode involving my grandmother's favourite talcum powder.'

He's human after all, thought Kate. I bet he'd be jolly good company in the right situation. Not that she was likely to get a chance to find out. Though just the thought made her feel oddly light-headed.

She realised he was speaking to her.

'If you're interested in the family history, there's a book here that you should read.' He crossed to a book case and searched along a shelf until he found what he was looking for. He slid the book from the shelf and laid it on the table.

Kate moved closer. She could see that it was

very old. The cover was faded brown leather and the pages, yellowed with age, showed signs of having been read many times over the years.

She glanced from the book to Ethan.

'This looks so fragile. Is it all right to handle it?'

'So long as we're careful. Go ahead. Open it.'

She looked down at the cover again. She was almost afraid to touch it in case it fell to pieces. Tentatively, she stroked a finger across its surface and had the strangest feeling of being suspended in time. This book was clearly something very special and she was amazed that she was being allowed to see it.

She was also acutely aware of Ethan standing behind her, watching her. She didn't need to turn her head to know that he was close. Every nerve ending was screaming the fact.

She drew a deep breath and carefully opened the book.

'Oh.' She gasped with delight.

Written on the first page, in neat copperplate handwriting, were the words, Florence Amelia Cade. Journal. 1796.

She turned to Ethan. 'This is beautiful. Who is she?'

'Florence was Jacob's wife. Sadly this is the only one of her journals to survive, though I believe she kept one for many years. There's an entry somewhere that is relevant to what we were just talking about, if I can find it.'

Before she could move to one side, he was

bending forward to turn the pages. He was so close, they were almost touching. His breath was warm on her neck and she shivered a little as it whispered across her ear. The male scent of him was intoxicating. Filling her head. Firing her senses. He must surely be able to hear the thump of her heart as the blood drummed through her veins.

She'd never believed in love at first sight. But lust at first sight? That must be what she was feeling.

'Here it is.' He pointed to the page and, as he did so, his arm brushed against hers, sending her pulse racing up another notch.

She forced her concentration back to the book and Florence's neat writing.

Since Mr Pitt took it into his head to impose taxation on powder, Jacob has taken to wearing his own hair and I have to confess that I much prefer it as I cannot but think that powdering must be bad for the health. I am of the firm opinion that it does much to improve his appearance.

She laughed. 'Was there really a tax on powder?'

'Apparently so.' He turned back to the papers he had been studying when she came in. 'I'm afraid I really must get on but feel free to stay and read. Just leave the book on the table when you've finished.'

CHAPTER 4

E than collected the papers he needed for Harry Crawford and put the rest away. It was time he turned his mind back to work and away from Kate McKenzie.

He'd been surprised to find that what had started as a conscious effort to be nice to her had all too easily developed into something quite different.

He had actually enjoyed her company. Enjoyed talking to her. Her interest in Hanging Cross and its history seemed genuine and he found himself wishing they could carry on talking about it. It was just as well he had work to do, otherwise he might have been tempted - and who knew where that might lead.

Hanging Cross was his life. Nothing meant as much to him, which was hardly surprising considering the amount of work he had put into restoring it. If it hadn't been for his father's untimely death - fortuitous might be a better word, his alter-ego whispered - there might not have been anything left to save. Even now, after more than fifteen years, he could not forgive him for his neglect of the estate.

Women and alcohol had ruled his father's life and drained the family fortune. How his mother had lived with the affairs and the drinking, he had never been able to understand. He had been away at school most of the time but the signs had been there for him to see every holiday when he came home. The sadness in his mother's eyes. The deepening lines at the corners of her mouth. Her quiet toleration of a life that became harder to bear with each new year.

Even then, as a schoolboy, he had vowed that when he fell in love, his marriage would be everything his parents' was not.

Only it hadn't worked out like that.

And he wasn't going to fall into the same trap again.

He glanced across the room to where Kate was sitting in an armchair by the window, her head bent over the book. Her hair had fallen forward, hiding her face. That beautiful hair that had haunted him from the first moment he had seen it as it tumbled out from beneath that absurd hat. The light from the window picked out golden highlights which seemed to dance in the rich copper colour that was so familiar to him. He itched to run his hands through it. To push it back from her face. To wrap it round his fingers and tilt her head backwards so that he could cover her mouth with his, taste her lips. Kiss her until she was breathless.

He shook himself. This would not do. There was no way he was going to get involved with her. In any case, he was still married.

He dragged his gaze away. That the attraction was mutual, he had no doubt. He had been acutely aware of her reaction as he had leaned across her to look at the book. That charge in the air between them had been unmistakeable. He knew the situation could easily get out of control unless he was very careful and he had every intention of being just that. He would be polite and friendly and that was all. Easy enough to say. The question was, how did he convince his hormones to co-operate?

But right now Crawford was waiting for him and he was already late.

§

Kate watched as Ethan collected his papers and left the library. Yet again, she was puzzled by his change of manner. Was this really the same man who, up to now, had been giving every indication that he disliked her and wanted as little as possible to do with her? Perhaps he had an identical twin? But hat was the sort of thing that happened in fiction - not in real life.

Yet there had been no mistaking the chemistry between them as they looked at the book together. She had felt the thrill when his arm had brushed hers and she was certain he had felt it, too.

Don't read anything into it, she warned herself. He could be back to his usual charm-less self tomorrow. And, in any case, she was off men. Wasn't she?

She pushed him out of her mind and glanced at her watch. She didn't have much time. It would soon be lunch and then Vanessa would be waiting for her. She returned to Florence's journal. Turning the pages, she became lost in a world that had existed more than two hundred years ago.

Then her pulse quickened as an entry leapt from the page.

We were almost discovered today. Jacob tells me a preventive officer happened by the chapel as a cargo was being stowed. I believe he had no suspicion but was merely patrolling the beach. All was quickly concealed and Jacob made so bold as to invite him to join them at prayer, at which the officer made a hasty departure and all was well.

Could that be the chapel Vanessa was telling her about, where she and her brother, Charles, had played?

Tonight, all will be carried up to the house. Tis well the ponies are so sure-footed as the recent heavy rains have rendered the path quite treacherous.

So there was a path from the chapel up to the house. Did it still exist? Florence's journal entry suggested the chapel was near the beach, in which case the path had to lead up the cliff to the house. And, as the smugglers wouldn't want to draw attention to it, it would almost certainly be well concealed.

And Kate had a pretty good idea of where that path might be.

That faint suggestion of a little-used path through the bracken that she could see from her bedroom window.

There wasn't time now, but as soon as she could she would investigate. Right now, she must go and eat.

She discovered that lunch was an informal meal laid out in the kitchen with everyone eating as and when they had time and Kate was surprised to find herself disappointed to see that Ethan had not yet returned from his appointment. She'd been looking forward to continuing their earlier conversation and had hoped for an opportunity to talk to him about the smuggling. Always assuming he was still in friendly mode, of course.

She didn't feel inclined to ask Ruby, who was as distant as ever.

She grabbed a sandwich, shared the crusts with the dogs - much to Ruby's disapproval - and went off to begin her afternoon session with Vanessa.

'Ah, there you are, Kate. Have you eaten?'

'I have. Thank you.' She hesitated, then asked, 'Vanessa, how can I persuade Ruby to stop calling me Miss?'

'I doubt you can. She's a stickler for what she calls, 'knowing her place'. I often think she should have been born a hundred years ago. She insists on calling Ethan 'Master', you know.

'Yes, I'd noticed. I thought it was rather odd.'

'I suppose it's tradition. As far back as Jacob, the head of the house has always been called Master. I don't know why it's lasted this long. In fact, I'm sure that Ruby is the only one who actually uses the title any more. Between you and me,' she grinned, ' I think Ethan quite likes it.'

Kate grinned back. 'Yes, somehow I can believe that.'

'Well, I shall leave you to make friends with that contraption next door while I work out how to extricate my heroine from the rather nasty fix she seems to have got herself into.'

She handed Kate the tape machine.

'Shout if you need anything. I shall either be in here or in my sitting room.'

Kate moved to her own room and sat down at her desk, relieved that at least the computer was up to date.

Then she jumped as the door opened and Vanessa peered round it.

'I nearly forgot,' Vanessa said. 'Apparently Helen is out of action and Ethan tells me the agency can't find him a temp. Not for a few days, anyway. So I suggested he might like you to help him out. I thought we could share you. Just for a little while, until he finds someone else. That's if you don't mind, of course. He's thinking about it.'

Then, without giving Kate a chance to say anything, she was gone.

Mind! As the door closed behind Vanessa, Kate closed her eyes and took a deep breath. Working for Ethan was positively the last thing she felt like doing.

Despite his friendly manner towards her that morning, there was no guarantee it would last and, judging from his mood when he was on the phone earlier, he could turn out to be the boss from hell. On top of which, the thought of being in the same room as him, in such close proximity to all that virile masculinity, was enough to turn her knees to jelly. How could she possibly concentrate on work in such a situation?

Off men, she might be. Off Ethan Cade, she clearly was not. However hard she tried to convince herself otherwise, she could not deny it. She was in lust with the man.

It went against all her good intentions. All her common sense. But then, when had common sense ever had anything to do with something as unpredictable as physical desire?

And now, she was being asked to work with him. In his office. In close contact. Shut in the same room together for hours. Her imagination - not to mention her hormones - were working overtime. It would be impossible.

Vanessa seemed to think it was a fait accompli. Had Ethan agreed? Somehow, she imagined he would be about as keen on the arrangement as she was. For quite a different reason, of course.

She fired up the computer. While it loaded, she

gazed out of the window in front of her, imagining how it would be if, instead of here in Vanessa's room, she was in the estate office now. With Ethan sitting at his own desk across the room. Or standing beside her, leaning across her as he had in the library. Brushing his arm against hers. Breathing his warm male breath across her ear and down her neck. She shivered. How on earth would she be able to concentrate on work?

The computer beeped that it was ready. Kate shook herself, put on the headphones, slotted the tape into the machine and pressed the play button. As her fingers typed, she slipped into auto mode, her mind going into freefall, bombarded by thoughts of Ethan and of Hanging Cross.

She loved it here. She was sure she was going to enjoy working for Vanessa and she didn't want to do anything that might jeopardise that. She knew she had no obligation to work for Ethan. She was contracted to Vanessa. But, on the other hand, would it really hurt to help out? Just for a few days? That's if he wanted her, of course. In all probability, he would turn down the offer anyway.

§

The next morning, Ethan's mood was deteriorating steadily. He dropped the day's post on top of the mounting pile of paperwork on his desk, and swore.

He was between a rock and a hard place.

The agency hadn't been able to find him a

temp and there was no way he could cope without help. The only immediate solution was to accept Vanessa's suggestion; which was the very last thing he wanted to do. Being friendly and polite to Kate McKenzie for an hour or so every now and then was all very well. Maintaining that over several hours in the close confines of the office was another matter altogether.

It had only been with great reluctance and, he had to admit, rather bad grace, that he had finally given in. Vanessa could be remarkably persuasive when she put her mind to something and he'd had to agree she had a point. He really had no good reason to refuse.

If he was honest, he knew his attitude was totally unreasonable. He had known the girl for little more than two days, during which time they had spent only a few hours together, yet she had got under his skin in a way he wouldn't have believed possible. But, of course, he knew why. If only she didn't …

No. He didn't even want to think about that.

He dragged his mind back to business. He was surprised that Kate had fallen in with Vanessa's suggestion and had agreed to work for him in the mornings while Vanessa dictated and he had grave doubts about the wisdom of allowing it.

He had no doubt she would be efficient. What he doubted was his own ability to keep his mind on work when his body would have other ideas entirely. A doubt that was soon confirmed.

There was a tap on the door and he looked up as Kate walked in. Her glossy hair was caught back from her face in a tortoiseshell clip. She was dressed in a neat skirt and a plain long-sleeved top in some dark green silky material that should have looked smart and business-like but merely served to accentuate her slender figure and offer tantalising suggestions of what might lie beneath.

He fought down the sudden rush of desire that surged through him. Get a hold, he told himself. Concentrate on work.

His voice was a growl as he wished her good morning.

'Good morning.' She smiled back at him.

God, if she continued to smile at him like that, he wasn't going to last the morning. His best bet was to explain to her what he wanted her to do and then get himself out of the office and leave her to it. The less time they spent together, the better. Be calm. Be polite, he told himself, and just get on with work.

'Well, here I am,' she said. 'What would you like me to do?'

His mind flew off at a tangent. His imagination went into overdrive.

'Perhaps you could start by opening the post?' He was relieved to hear that his voice sounded more or less normal. 'There seems to be rather a lot of it, I'm afraid.'

§

Faced with a situation she couldn't easily avoid, Kate was determined to make the best of it. She would be friendly and cheerful and hope that he would be the same. In that way, maybe the two of them could rub along together for a few days without too much stress.

Ethan was dressed for the office in navy chinos and a blue cord shirt that emphasised his dark good looks and she was glad she had decided to wear something smart herself. He looked just as attractive as he did in riding clothes, but then he was the kind of man who would look good in almost anything. She shook her head and concentrated her mind on work.

Settling herself at his secretary's desk, she began to tackle the stack of letters. She sorted them into piles - junk, personal, business and entered them into the post book.

'Shouldn't I know a bit about what you do?' she asked. 'In case I get phone calls or anything?'

He leant back in that black leather chair that gave him such an appearance of power - maybe that was his intention? - and looked at her.

'Yes, I suppose you should. The main business is DeskSpace.'

She'd heard of it. A nationwide chain of extremely successful high-quality serviced offices.

'You own that?' she was impressed.

'I made some decent property deals before the market collapsed and used the profits to set up DeskSpace. I still own a few of those properties.

Mainly hotels, conference centres, that sort of thing. I'll let you have a list of them in case you have any queries.'

'I take it you don't run everything from here?'

He actually smiled. Slightly. 'I wish I could. But, no. I have offices in London.'

'Then don't you have another secretary or typist that could be seconded to you temporarily?'

'It would mean re-shuffling people in London and I'd rather not create problems for them if I can avoid it. I think I'll wait and see what the agency can provide before I bring anyone out from there.'

'Do you spend much time in London?'

'No more than I have to. I have a flat in town that I use if I have to stay any length of time but I prefer working here and I'm fortunate enough to be able to indulge myself as far as that goes.'

'I can understand that. I was glad to leave London, myself. Mind you, I bet your place is a bit different to my Clapham bed-sit. I used to promise myself that, one day, when I got a big enough rise, I'd find a flat near the park where I could pretend I was in the country.' She shrugged. 'Only I never did get the rise. This place is so peaceful and beautiful it makes me realise how much I missed the countryside.'

Abruptly, he swung forward on his chair and opened the file on his desk. 'Which is why I come here to work. Work being the operative word, Miss McKenzie.'

'Pardon? Oh, sorry.' There it was again. That

sudden change of mood. His voice had changed. Become icy. Talk about making it clear that she was here to work and not to socialise. Huh!

She carried on opening the letters.

Then she paused, puzzled.

'Sorry to interrupt - again,' she couldn't quite resist the little dig, 'but there's one here addressed to Mrs Cade.' She studied the envelope. 'I expect they mean Miss Cade. It's probably for Vanessa. I think it's only junk mail and these companies are always getting names wrong, aren't they.'

Ethan looked up. 'It will be for my wife.' His voice, now, was flat; devoid of expression.

His wife? This was the first she had heard of him being married. But then, she supposed, why shouldn't he be? But then again, if he was, where was his wife? Why hadn't he mentioned her? Come to that, why hadn't Vanessa mentioned her? The questions sped through her head.

And why should she feel such a thud in the pit of her stomach? It wasn't as though she and Ethan were an item. Or even friends. It wasn't as if she even liked him that much. So why did she feel something curl up and shrivel inside her at the news?

'You're married? I didn't know.'

Something must have shown in her face, or her voice.

'Why should you? Don't looked so shocked. I haven't strangled her and buried her in the cellar. She left of her own accord and I'm currently in the process of divorcing her.'

'Oh.'

'I would have mentioned it but I assumed you already knew. Obviously, that's one part of the family story Vanessa hasn't told you.' There was a note of sarcasm in his voice.

'No, she hasn't.' She was flustered and didn't quite know what to say. So she just said, 'I'm sorry.'

'No need to be. It all happened some time ago.'

'What shall I do with the letter?'

'I'll give you the address of her solicitor. Anything that comes in the post for her can be forwarded to him.'

'Right.'

She finished sorting the post in silence, her mind playing over their conversation, her curiosity more aroused than ever. She dropped the junk in the waste basket then walked over to Ethan's desk and placed the letters needing his attention in a neat stack in front of him.

He flicked through the pile and frowned. 'There are some here that will need answering. How's your shorthand?'

'Ah, I was hoping you wouldn't ask me that.'

He raised an eyebrow, quizzically and her heart flipped. 'That bad, eh?'

'No. Not bad. Just a bit rusty. So long as you don't speak too fast, I can keep up.' I hope, she added silently. For some reason she couldn't quite understand, she needed to prove herself to him. Show him that she was as capable as the secretary she was standing in for. But he wasn't looking pleased and Kate decided she must have imagined that flash of amusement in his eye.

Impatiently he glanced at his watch. 'Okay. I was under the impression that you were a competent secretary. But if that's the best you can manage, I guess it will have to do. I have an appointment in an hour so let's cut the chat and get down to work, shall we.'

And, just at that moment, Kate's mobile rang. Blast. She was sure she had turned it off before coming into the office. But clearly she had not.

Ethan glared at her.

She grimaced, wondering whether she should leave it or answer it.

'Well do something with it for Heaven's sake,' Ethan growled.

'Sorry.' She grabbed her bag and took out the offending phone. The caller's number came up on the display.

Richard again.

She killed the call and turned off the phone. How on earth was she going to stop him phoning her?

'Nothing important,' she said dropping the phone back into her bag.

'Than perhaps we can get on with these letters? That's if you are quite ready, of course?

Kate gritted her teeth. So much for her good intentions. The man was impossible. He was lucky she didn't throw something at him. She was, after all, doing him a favour.

Don't let him get to you, she told herself. Just because he was behaving like a boor, didn't mean she had to lower herself to his level.

She grasped pad and pencil, looked him in the eye, and sent him a silent challenge.

Ethan read through the first letter and began dictating.

Only half his mind was on what he was saying. The other half was busy reproving himself for losing it again.

Why did she have to go comparing her bed-sit with his flat? Drawing attention to the difference in their... in their... Hell, call a spade a spade... In their financial status. As if she was...

He forced himself to concentrate on dealing with the letters.

... as if she was angling for something? Looking for a handout? Don't be ridiculous. Not everyone was like Caroline.

She seemed distracted. He had the impression that she had been disturbed by the phone call and wondered why. He almost asked her if everything was okay. Then decided it was none of his business and said nothing.

After an hour of dictating, the urgent correspondence was dealt with.

He'd pushed her hard but she'd given as good as she got. She had spirit. He liked that. In fact, he was finding there was a lot about Kate that he liked. If only …

'I have a meeting with my estate manager which shouldn't take long,' he told her. 'I hope to be back here before you leave. When you've finished those letters, perhaps you would deal with the filing? It shouldn't be difficult. You'll find Helen has everything clearly labelled and organised.'

'Yes, sir.'

Had he imagined it? Or had she been about to salute? He could have sworn she had started to raise her arm, then thought better of it. Lord, was he that bad? It was all he could do to stop himself smiling. How could he feel so antagonistic towards her one minute and want to smile at her the next? He wished he knew. And he wished he could work out what to do about it.

He looked down at the desk and concentrated on collecting his things and packing his briefcase. Having got his face under control, he took his jacket from the back of his chair and shrugged into it, picked up his case, and headed for the door.

'See you in about an hour.'

Just as he was leaving the room, he glanced back.

She was stretching her arms above her head, easing tension from her neck.

All thoughts of his meeting with Crawford vanished and the image burned on his mind as he headed for the Land Rover, was that of dark green silk moulding itself enticingly to softly out-thrust breasts.

CHAPTER 5

As soon as Ethan had left the office, Kate took out her mobile and began to dial Richard's number. Somehow, she had to stop him calling. Then she had second thoughts and cancelled it and swiftly keyed in a text message instead.

We are finished. Please don't phone me again. Kate.

Okay, so it was taking the coward's way out but she really would prefer not to have to talk to him. Also, the bluntness of it might just get the message home.

She pressed send.

Now she needed something to take her mind off it and there was nothing quite so mind-numbing as filing. It was a job she really disliked but it had to be done and Ethan sure as hell wasn't going to do any himself. Of that she was quite certain. She had no doubt that in his view filing was a job for menials not masters. But it was just what she needed right now. Something easy and non-demanding.

Just as soon as she'd typed up the letters.

She was really beginning to wonder why she was making such an effort to get along with Ethan when all he seemed to want was to get the job done and see the back of her. But deep down she sensed there was more to it than that. There had been moments when the air between them was alive with tension; and it wasn't just his animosity. It was as if they were on opposite ends of a coiled spring, being inexorably drawn together until, with a huge effort of will, they managed to pull apart, just for the whole process to begin again. And she was finding it both mentally and physically exhausting.

It was a relief to be on her own for a while and to be able to collect her thoughts coolly, without his presence sending her adrenalin levels sky-high. When he was around, she felt as though she was on a permanent caffeine overdose.

She dropped the finished letters onto his desk for signing.

Then she heaved a tray of papers across to the table next to the filing cabinets and began sorting them into piles. Some of the projects he was involved with looked really interesting, especially those that concerned Hanging Cross. She hadn't realised how large the estate was and it was clear he had put a good deal of effort into improving the property. What a pity he was such a pain to work for. She could have enjoyed it had he been more approachable.

She slipped a folder of plans for the renovation of a row of cottages into the filing drawer and, as she did so, she noticed one labelled Jacob's Chapel. Across the front of the folder it was marked Project Cancelled. Intrigued, she pulled it out and opened it. Could this refer to the chapel she had read about in Florence's journal?

Inside was a drawing of the disused chapel and a map showing its position somewhere down the cliff near the sea. She looked closer. There was something familiar about the area shown on the map and as she traced its position with her finger she realised that, as she had suspected, the path leading down the cliff was almost certainly an extension of the one she had seen from her bedroom window. The path had looked overgrown and impassable, but her curiosity was aroused and she determined to explore further as soon as she had the opportunity.

She flicked through the rest of the contents and found a set of plans for the conversion of the chapel into a dwelling, dated about three years ago. She was intrigued to see that someone had scored through them with a red pen. Heavily. Angrily. Could it have been Ethan who had dealt so savagely with it? If so, why?

Engrossed in studying the plans, she didn't hear the door open.

'What the hell are you doing with that?'

Startled, she dropped the folder and its contents spilled out on to the floor. She turned and looked up.

Ethan stood in the doorway, his expression as black and forbidding as she had ever seen it.

'Who gave you permission to look at that?' His voice was thick with emotion.

He was angry but Kate sensed another emotion there as well. She saw the slight flush that ringed his neck beneath his collar. Whatever it was, had affected him deeply.

She stooped to pick up the scattered papers.

'It was in the filing drawer. I didn't realise it was private.' She tried to keep her voice level and calm. 'I'm sorry if I've …'

He interrupted her. 'Just leave it.,' he snapped. 'I'll deal with it later.'

Kate scooped the papers up in one bundle. The old adrenalin was working overtime and she could feel her temper rising again.

'There's no need to be rude,' she said. 'I was merely following your orders and dealing with the filing. I wasn't aware I was expected to do it with my eyes shut.'

She dropped the papers on the table and kicked the drawer closed with her foot. This man managed to get under her skin like no other man she had known. She wasn't even employed by him. She was doing him a favour and this was how he acted. He really was quite insufferable.

She swept her jacket from where she had left it on the back of the chair, and headed for the door.

'I take it you have finished with my services?'

she said.

Her heart was pounding. Her hands shaking. She was on an adrenalin high. If she didn't work some of it off she would burst.

Somehow, she still had to get through the afternoon with Vanessa. Could she control her hands sufficiently to be able to type? At the moment, she doubted it. What she needed was coffee. Good and strong. Or, even better, a good stiff drink.

Wrong.

What she really needed was a punch bag. With his face printed on it.

She made her way to the kitchen, thinking she would have an early lunch, then perhaps there would be time for a quick walk round the garden before she had to start work with Vanessa.

It looked as though she wasn't the only one planning an early meal. When she reached the kitchen, Vanessa was already sitting at the table, dogs at her feet, hands wrapped round a large mug of soup. Her face was drawn and her hair, once again escaped from its clip, looked as though she had spent the morning running her hands through it. It seemed they had both had a difficult few hours.

Kate fixed on a smile and tried to look cheerful. 'Hi, Vanessa.'

The dogs turned their heads towards her, thumping their tails on the floor in greeting, before resuming their positions, eyes fixed hopefully on the table, patiently waiting for titbits.

'Hello, Kate. How did you get on?'

Kate grimaced inwardly. Absolute purgatory. He's rude, disagreeable, impossible. And gorgeous. Almost as though there were two of him. Perhaps he had a split personality. That would certainly account for a lot.

'Okay,' she said out loud, trying to sound as though everything had been just fine.

'That's good. Ruby's left a pan of soup on the Aga. Help yourself.'

Kate filled a mug with hot carrot soup and took it back to the table. She thought Vanessa looked tired.

'How's the writing going?' she asked.

Vanessa shrugged. 'Not good. It's been one of those mornings when the words just refuse to flow. In fact, I'm not sure that I have much for you to do this afternoon.' She looked at Kate. 'Actually, you look as though you could do with a break yourself. What do you say to a couple of hours off while I try and make some progress? Go and have a rest or something? Recharge your batteries.'

Just what she needed. And she knew exactly what she could do.

'That would be lovely. Do you think I could go for a walk? Take the dogs perhaps?'

Tails thumped again at the word 'walk' and bottoms shuffled excitedly on the floor.

'I don't see why not. I'm sure Ethan wouldn't mind. I think he's out for the afternoon anyway.

Some meeting or other. Where did you think of going? There are some lovely walks through the woods. Some of the paths take you up onto the moor but I wouldn't go too far on your own until you get to know the area a bit better.'

'I won't. I thought I might explore the grounds.'

'Well I don't suppose you'll get lost doing that, but the dogs know their way home if you do lose your way.' She pushed back her chair and stood up. 'I shall get back to work and leave you to it. I'll see you in a couple of hours.'

Kate finished her soup and rinsed the mug in the sink.

The dogs' leads hung by the back door. 'I suppose I'd better take these.' She unhooked them from the pegs and Belle and Otto leapt to their feet, panting with excitement. 'Though I don't suppose I shall need them, you being such well-trained dogs.'

Tails wagged frantically.

'Come along then. Heel.'

To her amazement, they both fell in beside her.

'Goodness, you are well trained, aren't you. But then the 'Master' wouldn't settle for anything less, would he?'

They barked their agreement.

'Okay, let's go along the terrace, shall we and see if we can find the path from there.'

She crossed the cobbled yard and turned round the corner of the house to where the terrace began.

She followed it past the high windows of the hall, the dogs padding along beside her, nails tapping on the paving stones, until she reached the far end. She looked up and could see her own bedroom window. This was where Ethan had been standing when she had looked down on him from her bedroom window on her first evening.

The view from here was incredible. It was the first time she had really stood and looked at it properly. She could see right across the lawns to the edge of the cliff and, beyond that, the sweep of the bay as it curved between two rocky headlands. The tide was out, exposing the shingle beach which dropped in a series of steeply shelving steps down to the sea's edge.

She could have stood there all day, absorbing its beauty. But she had only a short time and she still had to find the path. It had been clearly visible from her bedroom window but everywhere looked quite different down here at ground level and it was a while before she found it. It was surprisingly well concealed among scrub and bracken.

'Okay, dogs. Here it is. Let's go.'

At first, the path followed the contour of the hill and, for a hundred metres or so, the going was fairly level, though in places the thickets of bracken were so dense she had a job to push her way through and straggling brambles caught at her clothes. Rowan and gorse, their growth stunted by the fierce winds, nevertheless grew high enough to prevent her seeing more than a few feet in front of her. There were moments when she feared she had lost the track but the dogs, bounding along in front of her, always seemed to find it again.

'I hope you two know where you're going,' she told them.

Then the path dog-legged, and she was out of the bushes and into the open. The view was stunning. In front of her, the rocky crags of the headland sloped towards the sea. To her left, the path zigzagged steeply down the side of a precipitous cliff to the beach, fifty feet below.

'Wow.' She stopped and stared. It seemed impossible that even the sure-footed Exmoor ponies could have made it up this cliff. But this surely had to be the path that Florence referred to in her journal. Everything fitted in with the map she had seen in the folder.

She turned and looked behind her. She could just see the house at the top of the hill. No wonder the view from up there was so incredible.

The dogs were watching her, panting, eager to be moving on.

'Philistines. You've no sense of beauty,' she told them. 'Come on then.'

Her foot slipped as she stepped forward. She would need to be careful. The path here was completely exposed to the weather from the sea and the ground was wet and muddy. It was also much steeper. Here and there, large rocks had been dug into the slope to form rough steps but these, too, were smooth and slippery with moisture.

The dogs ran backwards and forwards, waiting for her, urging her on, leading the way as she trod warily, not taking any chances with her footing, until she was almost at the bottom. The last few feet were so steep that she found herself moving faster and faster until she was running, unable to stop, out onto the shingle beach, to where the foaming breakers sucked and pounded at the pebbles before rolling over to break in a splash of sun-brightened foam that fanned out towards her, infinitely thinned, before being dragged back to begin the cycle again. She could smell the salt in the air and taste it on her lips. It was exhilarating.

She spread her arms and spun round as if encompassing the whole of the bay. Holding her face up to the sky. Feeling the sea breeze in her hair. This must be the most beautiful place on earth. And, more than anything, she wanted to stay here. Whatever it took to keep her job, she would do it.

Even as far as getting along with Ethan Cade.

Which reminded her. She had only two hours and it was going to take much longer to climb back up the cliff than it had to come down it.

And she still had to find the chapel.

She turned to call the dogs. But the beach was empty and there was no sign of them.

Darn it.

'Otto! Belle!'

Where on earth had they gone to?

The shingle scrunched and shifted beneath

her feet as she crossed the shingle, re-tracing her steps towards the path, calling as she went. There was no sign of them - and no sign of where the chapel might be, either. Then she noticed another path leading off from the one she had come down, but at sea-level, hugging the foot of the cliff as it turned inland.

She followed it and the land began to rise again, but gently. The vegetation became thicker and more lush.

She was beginning to wonder if she was going the wrong way, when she heard one of the dogs bark.

She turned off the path in the direction of the sound and found herself in dense undergrowth and trees. Great drifts of ferns and nettles covered the ground. Ash and birch saplings competed for space with stunted mature trees. It was dark and shady. Then she turned a corner and there it was.

The chapel was so well hidden that she would almost certainly have missed it had it not been for the dogs. It was a perfect hiding place for smugglers.

The building seemed in remarkably good condition considering its age. Its grey stone walls and slate roof were still largely intact. Some of the windows had lost their glass and had been boarded but the heavy oak door still hung in place beneath the arched stone porch.

Gingerly, she pushed it open and stepped inside.

The floor was flagged with the same smooth grey stone that had formed the rough steps on the path. Simple wooden pews lined each side of the central aisle. The atmosphere was cool and silent. And haunting. As though it hid a hundred secrets. Which, she thought, it probably did.

She cast her mind back to Florence's journal. Where, she wondered, had they hidden the contraband? If only she had more time but, looking at her watch, she realised she was going to have to leave if she wasn't going to be late getting back to the house.

As she left the gloom of the interior and came out into the light, the dogs re-appeared at her side.

'About time,' she told them. 'Where do you think you've been?'

They just looked at her, panting with exertion, tongues lolling, tails wagging.

'Come on. Time to go home.'

She found her way back to the beach and began climbing the cliff path. It looked pretty daunting from down here - a long way to the top. It was much steeper than she had realised and she was soon flagging. Barely half way up she had to stop and rest. Bending forward, hands on knees, she took some deep breaths. Her heart was pounding. Her pulse way up. Her thighs ached and she had a stitch in her side. Clearly, she wasn't as fit as she'd thought she was.

She straightened and braced herself to resume the climb. How far was it to the top? She looked up, trying to judge the distance, and ...

'Oh my God. I don't believe it.'

Standing at the top of the cliff watching her was Ethan.

Just her luck. She was hot and sweaty. Her hair was a mess and she just knew that her face was beetroot red with exertion. It wasn't that she actually cared what he thought of her appearance. Don't you? whispered a treacherous little voice inside her. Of course she didn't. Why on earth should she care? You know why, the treacherous voice mocked.

She squared her shoulders and pressed on. She would get to the top without stopping again if it killed her.

Otto and Belle had already raced ahead, excited at seeing their master, and all three were now watching her progress.

What sort of mood would he be in now? she wondered. She had been feeling so good after her walk. The exertion had worked off all the stress of the morning and she'd been ready to face the afternoon, a new woman.

What she wasn't ready to face, was Ethan Cade.

If anything, he was in an even worse mood than he had been that morning. That became obvious as soon she reached the top of the cliff. He glared at her, his face like thunder.

'What were you doing down there?'

So much for her hope that things might have

improved. She felt her hackles rise. 'I should have thought that was obvious. I was going for a walk.' She was still out of breath from the climb and the effort of breathing deeply helped to steady her.

'Why down there?' he demanded.

Stay calm, she told herself. Remember, you love it here. You want to keep this job.

'I was exploring. I'd been reading about the chapel in Florence's journal and I wanted to see it.'

She was shocked at the anger that blazed in his eyes.

When he spoke, his voice was icy. 'How dare you go there. You are never to go there again. Do you understand?'

She opened her mouth to protest but he cut in before she could speak.

'And why aren't you working?'

Oh! He was impossible. What was it to do with him? It was his aunt she was working for, not him.

'I was given some time off.' She willed herself to stay cool. 'Vanessa needed more time to get work ready for me so she told me to go out for a couple of hours.'

'She did?'

'Yes. She did. She thought I looked stressed and needed a break.'

'A break from what?'

He'd asked for it. 'From you,' she snapped.

'Don't be ridiculous. If you can't take the stress, you shouldn't be doing the work.'

'Hey, whose idea was it that I work for you? I

seem to remember it was you who asked me, not the other way round.'

'Actually, it was Vanessa's idea.'

Her control broke. 'Well it was a rotten idea.' She realised she was shouting but didn't care. 'Why she should think I would want to work for you, I can't imagine. You are the most high-handed, domineering, overbearing man I have ever had the misfortune to meet and I'm amazed that you can get anyone to agree to work for you.'

'You're right. It was a rotten idea. Maybe you just don't have what it takes.'

She could have hit him. Screamed at him. Stamped her foot. But she did none of those things because, to her dismay, she knew she was about to cry. She had to get away. Quickly.

'If that's what you think,' she flung at him, 'you can manage without me.'

Then she turned and walked away from him, head held high, bottom lip caught tightly between her teeth as she fought to maintain her self control.

§

Ethan remained where he was, watching Kate as she made her way back to the house, and told himself what a bastard he was.

He had spent the morning trying to concentrate on work when all he could think about was her. She haunted him. No matter how hard he'd tried to get out her out of his mind he'd kept hearing her voice; seeing her face; imagining what it would be like to run his hand through her hair, down her arms, beneath that silky green top she had been wearing that morning.

Enough. He had to stop thinking of her like that or he would go mad.

He could kick himself for upsetting her just now, for speaking to her as he had. He couldn't understand the effect she had on him. He seemed totally incapable of acting normally with her. It was as if he could only experience extremes of emotion. There was no comfortable middle ground.

He wanted her. He was honest enough to admit that. But he couldn't allow it to happen. It would be history repeating itself.

If only she hadn't gone down there. He'd done his best to forget the place existed.

He realised he hadn't helped matters by giving her the journal to read, but, stupidly, he had forgotten it contained references to the chapel.

Then there had been the episode with the file in the office. She must have read some of it before he came in and found her. No wonder she was curious.

The dogs sensed his mood. One of them wined.

Absent-mindedly, he bent down and fondled their ears, and they snuffled and wriggled with pleasure.

'What am I going to do?' he murmured.

§

As soon as she was out of Ethan's sight, Kate broke into a run. She had to get back to the house, up to the privacy of her own room, before she lost control of the tears that were building up behind her eyes.

She reached her bedroom and closed the door behind her with a sigh of relief. Then she sat on the edge of the bed, dropped her head in her hands and allowed herself to sob away the tension that was racking her body.

Eventually, when it seemed she had no more tears to shed, she found a box of tissues and dried her eyes and blew her nose and walked across to the mirror to inspect the damage. It was not a reassuring sight.

Well that was a pretty stupid thing to do.

There was nothing like a good cry for releasing tension but how she envied those girls who could weep beautifully. Her face was blotchy and her eyes and nose were red and swollen. Definitely not fit to be seen in public.

She studied her ravaged reflection. Why do you let him get to you like this?

Good question. And she didn't know the answer.

You don't even like him. He's moody and rude.

He had been friendly and welcoming when they first met.

For five minutes.

He was the sexiest thing on two legs that she'd ever seen.

So you're in lust with him. Doesn't mean you have to like him.

I have to work with him.

No, you don't. Tell Vanessa you don't want to.

But I love being here. I don't want to lose my job.

No reason why you should. You're here to work for her not him.

Right. She'd do exactly that. She would tell Vanessa that it just wasn't possible for her to work with Ethan.

Decision made.

Now to repair the damage.

She stripped off her clothes and stood under the shower, enjoying the feel of the water sluicing through her hair and over her body, soothing and cleansing. *I'm going to wash that man right out of my hair.* She felt better already.

She towelled dry and dressed. Her face was almost back to normal. She applied some makeup and inspected the result. Not too bad. A bit pink and puffy round the eyes but maybe she could get away with saying it was hay fever. At this time of year? Maybe not. Well, perhaps no-one would notice anyway.

At least she wouldn't have to suffer another morning filing for the 'Master'.

'Here goes.'

She took a deep breath and opened the door

And just at that moment, her mobile began to ring.

CHAPTER 6

She hesitated. Should she answer it or leave it to pick up a message?

She looked at her watch. She had a few minutes before she needed to go. She closed the door and took her phone from her bag.

Richard, again! How long was he going to keep this up?

It was a ridiculous situation. She had lost count of the number of times he had tried to contact her. She had texted him; ignored him; tried to reason with him. Perhaps it was time to just be totally blunt.

Angrily, she punched the button to take the call and, without waiting for him to speak she snapped, 'Richard, this has got to stop.'

'Katie? Please, just listen to me for a minute.'

'I've listened to as much as I want to. There's nothing you can say that will make me change my mind about anything.'

'I want to say I'm sorry, that's all and …'

'Okay, you've said it.'

'Can't we still be friends, Katie?'

Kate groaned. That old chestnut. As if they could possibly remain friends after all this. 'No. We can't. Now, I have to go to work so I'm going to end this call and I don't want to hear from you again. Is that quite clear?'

'Katie …'

She cut him off and threw the phone down on the bed.

That was all she needed after the way today had gone so far. Now she was uptight and on edge again.

She just hoped that he would finally have got the message because his persistence was beginning to worry her. Perhaps she should tell Ethan and ask him what she should do. He was the kind of man who would know just how to deal with nuisance calls. But something made her hesitate.

She couldn't bring herself to ask him for help. He would be unbearably superior about it and, after all, Richard was no threat, merely a pain in the neck. She would sort it out herself.

Vanessa was waiting for her, looking inordinately pleased with herself. She looked up from where she was sitting on the sofa, and beamed. 'I'm afraid you are going to be busy, Kate. I've had an excellent afternoon. Look.' With a flourish, she held up two tapes. 'Two whole hours.'

She paused and frowned and Kate knew she wasn't going to get away with it.

'Is something wrong, Kate? Did you enjoy your

walk?'

Please don't let Vanessa be kind, she prayed, or I shall cry again. I know I will.

'I had a lovely walk. Thank you.' Perhaps if she ignored the first part of Vanessa's inquiry, she would drop it.

No such luck.

'Then why are you looking so miserable? What has happened?'

'Nothing much.' She tried to sound casual, as if it didn't matter in the slightest. 'Ethan and I have agreed that it's best if I stop working for him. That's all.'

'Really, Kate. I wasn't born yesterday.' She patted the seat next to her. 'Come and sit down and tell me about it.'

Kate sank into the soft cushion of the sofa, elbows on knees, cupping her chin in her hands, and took a deep breath.

'I walked down the cliff path to the beach and found the chapel.'

Vanessa's silence spoke volumes. After a moment, she said, 'Oh. I see.'

'Ethan was waiting at the top of the cliff when I got back. He was furious and I don't understand why.'

'No. There's no reason why you should.'

Kate looked at her. Perhaps now was the time to ask the question that had been bothering her almost since the day she'd arrived at Hanging Cross.

'Vanessa, is there something you're not telling me? Something I should know?'

Vanessa stood up and wandered across the room to stand at the window.

Kate waited. She sensed that Vanessa was thinking. Was she wondering what, or how much, to tell her?

Eventually, with a sigh, Vanessa turned to face her. 'You're right. It's only fair you should know. I suppose should have told you sooner but ...' she thrust her hands into the cavernous pockets of her long cardigan and leant back against the window sill, '... it's such a private matter, you see, and we've known you such a short time. But you have to live here so it's only right that you should understand.' She dug her hands further into her pockets and sighed deeply. 'But where to begin, I wonder,' she murmured.

Instinctively, Kate felt it had something to do with Ethan's wife.

'Is it connected with Mrs Cade?'

Vanessa looked surprised. 'You know about her?'

'I know that Ethan was married and is now getting a divorce.'

'He told you?'

'Only because there was a letter in the post that was addressed to Mrs Cade and I thought it might have been for you. I don't think he would have said anything otherwise.'

'No, maybe not. Well, that makes it easier. He

met Caroline about a year ago. No, it must be nearer eighteen months I should think. In a way I blame myself, although that's silly I know. You see, I had asked Ethan to escort me to a party. He hadn't wanted to go but I persuaded him and eventually he gave in. If I hadn't insisted on going, maybe they would never have met. She'd just come home from abroad, you see, and would probably have gone away again if it hadn't been for that chance meeting.

'Anyway, Caroline was something of a beauty. She flirted with him outrageously and he fell for her. Six month's later, they were married.'

'It sounds like a fairy-tale romance.'

'Except there was no happy ending. Soon after they returned from their honeymoon, Ethan discovered she was having an affair. The man was someone she had known for ages. In fact, the affair had been going on for months, long before she and Ethan met.'

'And she continued it afterwards?' Kate was horrified. 'How could she do that? That's so ... so cruel.'

'It turned out she had planned everything. She'd discovered that Ethan was wealthy and set out to snare him, fully intending to carry on with the affair. She apparently never had any intention of giving the other man up. When Ethan tackled her about it, she just laughed. She was quite happy to let him divorce her so long as she got a suitably large settlement. Which she did, of course.'

'But why? Surely no court would have supported her claim? Not in view of her behaviour?'

'Maybe not. But Ethan is too much of a gentleman to drag her through the courts, despite what she made him suffer. And too proud to want it all made public. He was dreadfully hurt and just wanted to see the back of her, and he was willing to pay handsomely to achieve it.'

'But where does the chapel come into it?'

'Ah, yes. The chapel.'

Vanessa shrugged herself away from the window and perched on the edge of the chair, facing Kate. She sat, hands clasped together between her knees, thinking. At last she said, 'That's where Ethan discovered them.'

Kate felt her heart drop to her stomach and rebound leaving her feeling slightly nauseous as the full significance of Vanessa's words hit her.

No wonder he'd been so angry to find she had been there. This explained so much. His moods. His reaction in the office when he had found her looking at the file.

Her heart went out to him.

'You mean, they were actually …?'

'I'm afraid so. She was quite blasé about it. Not an ounce of shame in her. Whereas Ethan refuses to talk about any of it. Keeps it all bottled up inside him.'

So now she knew. She could well believe he wouldn't want anyone to know about his wife's betrayal. He was not the sort to suffer fools gladly and would probably have died before allowing himself to be seen as one. She could quite understand why he had agreed to that settlement without a fight - and why he didn't talk about it. It was totally in keeping with his personality. It would have been a huge blow to his pride.

But in that case why had he told his aunt? Wouldn't he have kept the details to himself?

'But he talked to you?'

'Oh, no. He never speaks of it all.'

'Then how did you know?'

'Can't you guess?' A look of disgust passed across Vanessa's face. 'She told me. Caroline. She was quite brazen, almost bragging, about how she had 'hooked' him as she put it. Told me everything. I suppose she knew that Ethan would never have told me himself but just why she wanted me to know, I really have no idea. Maybe it was just spite. That would have been completely in character. Of course, he is now convinced that any woman who shows any interest in him will only be after his money.'

Another cog clicked into place. He hated her saying anything that related to her financial position. It hadn't registered at the time but, now, she could see it clearly. Her comment about having to buy a cheap car; life on a shoestring. Her remark about the difference between his flat in London and her Clapham bed-sit. All said in complete innocence on her part but he must have seen it as fishing, as if she was seeing him as a potential catch.

When she'd entered Vanessa's room, everything had seemed straight forward. She had made her decision and felt better for it.

Now, in light of what she had just learned, she was back on a rollercoaster of uncertainty.

Her mind played it over and over again throughout the rest of the day.

It was fortunate she was able to type almost without thinking about it, even though her concentration was elsewhere.

Dinner that evening was a difficult meal. Ethan's mood was not improved and he hardly said a word all through. None of them ate much, each lost in their own thoughts, which upset Ruby who huffed her displeasure at them, and Kate was relieved when she was finally able to retire to her room.

She curled up on the window seat and looked out at the garden. She was glad that Vanessa had explained the situation to her but the knowledge sat heavily and she felt uneasy about knowing something so personal about a man she'd met only a few days ago.

If only she was able to tell Ethan that she knew why he had been so angry. And that she understood. But would that help or would it only make matters worse? She had no way of telling.

He had gone to such great lengths to keep the matter quiet. How would he react if he knew

Vanessa had told her everything?

It made her own experience seem insignificant. She had believed herself in love with Richard and thought he had felt the same towards her. Okay, he hadn't actually told her he loved her, except when he wrote that message on the back of the photograph, but everyone did that, didn't they. People signed letters 'love from' all the time without actually meaning it. But he had behaved as though he loved her. She had been so confident he was going to ask her to marry him and when she'd discovered he was seeing someone else at the same time she had thought her heart would break.

If she had felt like that over Richard, how much worse it must have been for Ethan knowing that Caroline had married him, gone to bed with him, while all the time she had been sleeping with another man? Going from Ethan's bed to her lover's. And then to find out she had planned it all just to get his money. He must have been devastated.

No wonder he felt the way he did about the chapel. To find that his wife of a few weeks was having an affair must have been bad enough. But to actually discover them together. She couldn't think of anything more awful.

When she finally went to bed, she lay for a long while tossing and turning, unable to settle. She could not get Ethan out of her mind and when she did, finally, manage to sleep, he filled her dreams as well. So she slept fitfully and woke the following morning feeling tired and drained; but she had made up her mind about one thing.

If she could find a way of letting Ethan know she understood - a way that wouldn't seem patronising or damage his pride - then perhaps they could manage to rub along together amicably. They might never make it as far as being friends but it would be start.

§

Ethan looked surprised to see her when she knocked and walked into his office after breakfast. Hardly surprising when she thought of how they had parted the day before with her telling him that he could manage without her. Well, she was going to make up for it today. Whatever his mood, she was determined to try and break down some of the barrier that existed between them.

He had already started opening his post and paused, paper knife in hand, as she came in.

She smiled. 'Why don't you let me finish that?'

'I wasn't expecting you. I thought you weren't going to work for me any more?' He wasn't returning her smile, but at least he wasn't scowling, which was something.

She kept the smile going. 'I um … let's say I had second thoughts.'

'Well …' He gestured to the pile of letters and held out the opener. 'Thanks. I appreciate it.'

She gathered up the letters and took them over to her own desk. Automatically, she opened them, stamped them and entered them in the post book, but only half her mind was on the job. If she was going to say anything, it had to be this morning.

But what to say? How to begin? Could she somehow just casually drop the subject into the conversation? Ethan was bent over his desk, writing, lines of concentration furrowing his forehead. He was engrossed in his work and hardly likely to want to chat, so casual conversation didn't seem to be a possibility. Perhaps she should just jump in with both feet, apologise for going there, and see where that led.

She stamped the last letter and added it to the pile, then leant back in her chair. There was still all that filing to do that she hadn't completed yesterday. She wondered whether she should carry on with it. Better ask him first.

She cleared her throat.

Ethan looked up.

'I wondered if you wanted me to finish the filing,' she said. 'Of, course, if you'd rather I didn't - after yesterday, I mean - I'd quite understand.'

He stopped writing and leant back in his chair. 'I think we should try and put yesterday behind us, don't you? And, yes, thank you. If you would finish the filing I should be grateful.'

He was going to carry on working. She had to speak now or miss her chance.

'Ethan,' she blurted out, 'I'm sorry.' Not quite what she'd planned to say but at least it was a start. She had his attention.

'For what?' He held his pen poised over the paper, impatient to resume writing.

'For yesterday. For… going to the chapel.'

There. She'd said it.

But she just knew she was going to regret it as she watched his mouth set into a hard line and his eyes darken with anger.

She had to carry on before her courage failed her. She rushed the words out.

'If only I'd known before, I wouldn't have gone there. I was only curious because I'd read the entry in the journal about its connection with the smugglers, and then Vanessa had mentioned that she used to play there as a child. It all sounded so intriguing and romantic. And there didn't seem to be any harm in it. I had absolutely no idea that there was anything … that it was such a …' She trailed off, not knowing how to finish.

'Now you know differently.' His voice was low and rigidly controlled.

'That's what I'm trying to tell you.' Oh, dear. This was coming out all wrong. Not how she'd intended at all. She persevered. 'You see, I do know. Vanessa explained when …'

He cut in. 'You knew? And still you went there?' The words sliced out. Dangerous as a razor.

She fought down a momentary alarm. 'No, that was afterwards.' She stood up. 'Ethan, for heaven's sake, will you listen to me. When Vanessa saw me yesterday afternoon, after you and I had met on the cliff, she knew something was wrong and that's when she told me. But I swear I didn't know until then.'

'I see,' he snapped. 'So you've been discussing me behind my back?'

'Oh, you're impossible.' She raised her arms in a gesture of exasperation.

'Then maybe trying to work together was a mistake, after all.' He pushed the lid onto his pen and reached down for his briefcase. 'I have to go out. Don't bother with the filing.' He stood, scraping the chair back with his legs, and began shoving papers into his case.

So much for trying to make peace with the man. It seemed all she'd done was to make matters worse. Holding on to her temper by a thread, she picked up the pile of letters that needed his attention and put them down in front of him on his desk.

'While we're on the subject of filing, why didn't you say something when I found the folder about the conversion?'

She realised her hands were shaking and grasped the edge of his desk to steady herself, then jumped as he slammed his briefcase down and leaned towards her.

'Because I don't have to explain my private life to you, he growled.'

Their heads were so close, almost touching over the top of the desk, that she could feel the anger radiating from him, see the sparks in his eyes.

'I'm not asking you to, but you could have just said it was off limits or not safe or something. Anything. And I wouldn't have gone near the place.'

'I didn't think it was necessary.'

'So, I'm a mind reader, am I? How do you expect me to know if you don't tell me? There's no sign on the path saying 'No Entry'. There's no barrier across it.'

'If that's what it takes to keep you out, I'll put one put there,' he shouted.

'You do that!' she flung back.

'I ..,'

Kate had a sudden vision of how they must look - two grown people snapping at each other like a couple of school kids shouting 'will', 'won't', 'will', 'won't' - and had an irresistible urge to laugh.

'You were going to say, 'I will.' weren't you?' she spluttered.

Ethan's face was unreadable.

Oh, lord. Had she gone too far? Maybe she shouldn't be laughing but the situation really was too ridiculous. She held her breath and fought for control. A hair-trigger silence stretched between them.

Then the corner of his mouth twitched. His eyes crinkled and he actually smiled.

He lifted his arms in a gesture of submission. 'You're right. I was. Childish, wasn't it?'

He stood upright and thrust his hands into his trouser pockets. Kate watched the smile slowly fade and the shadows return to his eyes. He looked at her and, so softly she could hardly hear, said, 'How much did Vanessa tell you?'

She'd been hoping he wouldn't ask. On the other hand, it would be a relief to clear the air between them. How much would he want her to know? She could tell him she knew very little, which might be easier on his pride. On the other hand, she knew it was essential she was completely honest with him. What she absolutely mustn't do was in any way deceive him because, if he found out, he might see her as just another Caroline and she was surprised to discover just how much that would matter to her.

She spoke gently, trying to hide the sympathy that threatened to shake her voice. She was afraid he would only see it as pity and that, she knew, would be fatal.

'She told me your wife was having an affair with a man she had known before your marriage and that she was still seeing him. And that you discovered them together in the chapel.'

For a moment he didn't speak. Then, 'Is that all? What did she tell you about Caroline?'

He seemed to be probing. Looking for something. What was it he wanted her to say? What was he trying to find out?

'That was the gist of it. She didn't really say anything at all about Caroline except that she …' She took a calming breath. '… she probably only married you for your money.'

'No probably about it.' Ethan pounded one fist into the palm of his other hand, his face suddenly haggard with pain.

She longed to put her arms round him and comfort him but, instinctively, she knew that would not be wise. She had pushed her luck and got away with it but she had gone far enough. It was time to let things be.

§

Ethan turned away from her to face the window, fighting down the anger and hurt that was threatening to choke him. Would he never be able to think about it without feeling this almost uncontrollable rage? The memories were still so vivid, even after all this time.

'Ethan.' Kate's voice cut into his thoughts. 'You said you had to go out.'

He'd forgotten. The men would be waiting for him.

'Yes, you're right.' He forced his mind back to the present. 'I must get a move on. Look, I'm going to be a bit late back for lunch. Do you think you could ask Ruby to keep something warm for me?'

'Of course.'

She smiled as she spoke and he felt his breath catch in his chest. Her voice was so soft and gentle, as if she really cared about how he was feeling. But, damn it, he didn't want her pity. What he wanted was …

Don't go there, he warned himself. Don't even

think it.

He checked his case and shrugged into his jacket.

'Thanks. I'll see you later.'

He left the office feeling as though he had just gone several rounds with a champion heavyweight boxer. It might have been an emotional rather than a physical battle, but it had left him feeling bruised and drained and his adrenalin level was sky high. He needed exercise to work some of it off.

If he had time later, he would take a ride up to the moor. A good gallop might help to clear his mind of the image of Kate, with her silky hair and green eyes. An image that had begun to haunt him. An image that reminded him of all the things he would far rather forget.

He was out longer than he expected and there was only a couple of hour's daylight left by the time he stopped the Land Rover outside the house and cut the engine. He'd missed lunch but, if he got a move on, he could still be out and back in time for dinner.

He strode across the yard and into the kitchen. He could hear sounds coming from the pantry. Presumably Ruby.

'Ruby,' he called. 'I'm going for a ride but I'll be back in time to eat.'

The pantry door opened and out came ... the very person he had spent most of the afternoon trying to put out of his mind.

'Hello,' she said. 'Not Ruby, I'm afraid. Just me.'

'Kate. Do you know where Ruby is?'

'Sorry. Afraid not.'

'Not to worry. I'll leave her a note.'

'Did I hear you say you were going riding?'

His heart dropped. Surely she wasn't going to suggest coming with him?

But she was. He could read it in her expression.

'I don't suppose there's any chance of me going along? I've been dying to ask you if I could borrow a horse sometime.'

This was not at all what he had planned.

'I'm afraid that's not possible. The horses aren't suitable for novice riders.'

'Oh, but I'm not a novice. I was brought up on a farm don't forget. I've been riding all my life.'

He was acutely aware of the way her eyes were sparkling with excitement. Of how her whole face glowed with enthusiasm. And of how a small, treacherous part of him was in danger of giving in.

'Of course, I'm a bit out of practise,' she was saying, ' because there wasn't much opportunity while I was in London. But I went home once or twice a month and then I rode as much as I could find time for.'

She was like a child anticipating a treat. Her excitement was catching and he was disconcerted to find that the thought of her riding alongside him, eyes shining, hair flying in the wind, was suddenly extremely appealing.

What the hell. He couldn't think of any good

reason to refuse her. Not one that would sound reasonable to her, anyway. Except that his purpose in going for a ride was to try and clear his mind of her - not to have her there with him. But he could hardly tell her that.

'You'll have to be quick,' he said at last. 'We don't have much time.'

'Fantastic! I'll be fine as I am.' She indicated the trousers and padded jacket she was wearing. 'I just need to fetch some boots and a hat.'

'Right. I'll get changed and see you at the stables.'

CHAPTER 7

She was ready and waiting for him when he walked into the stable yard. He hesitated a moment, wondering which horse would be best for her.

'I think we'll put you on Bracken,' he decided, indicating a pretty chestnut mare. 'She's nice-natured but she'll run all day, so I hope you weren't exaggerating when you said you could ride well.'

'I think I can manage her,' she replied with a slight lift of her head.

There was that look again, as if she was challenging him, and he felt a frisson of something he couldn't quite identify shiver along his spine. Against the odds, he knew he was going to enjoy this ride.

He called to the stable lad who was busy filling hay nets prior to bedding down for the evening. 'Andy, tack up Bracken, will you. I'll see to Mack myself. And don't wait for us. I'll see to the horses when we get back.'

He led out his own sixteen-hand hunter and swiftly saddled him up. 'This could be an interesting outing, Mack,' he murmured, stroking the horse's silky nose as he slipped the bit between it's teeth and fastened the bridle straps. Then he sprang lightly into the saddle, checked his girths and waited as Kate did the same.

'Ready?' he called.

'Ready,' she called back. He could see her eyes sparkling with pleasure.

'Right. Let's go.'

He led the way out of the yard and up the combe, through the woods, the horses picking their way carefully over the stony ground, occasionally stumbling slightly as the way grew steeper. The path was narrow in places and they had to keep to single file.

He glanced over his shoulder and called to Kate.

'Everything okay?'

'Wonderful.'

She rode well, he thought. She had a good seat. Sat well in the saddle. He noted how firmly her legs gripped the mare's flanks. How her trousers stretched tightly over her thighs as she moved easily with the rhythm of her horse. He dragged his eyes away from her legs and forced himself to look where he was going. If he wasn't careful, his imagination was going to leap into overdrive. He kicked on, eager to reach the top so that he could give his horse its head.

Eventually, the path widened and they left the tree line, crested the hill and rode out on to the open moor.

§

Kate gasped with delight as she looked around. The mare was fidgety, fighting for her head. The wind was behind her and she wanted to run but Kate held her in.

'In a moment,' she told her, leaning forward and stroking the silky neck. First she wanted to drink in the beauty of the countryside. They were high up on the top of the moor and she could see for miles in every direction. She might be on top of the world. All around her she could look down on shadowy tree-clad valleys, steep sided, cutting deep into the hill sides, some dry, some glistening with rivers winding towards the sea. Rich purples and yellows of heather and gorse covered the high ground in a blaze of colour. It was breath-taking.

The faint scent of earth and crushed grass drifted on the breeze that ruffled her hair and made the skin of her face tingle with its crispness.

She turned in the saddle. Behind her, she could just make out the road she had driven along on the day of her arrival, and the crossroads where she had turned down to the house.

Ethan pulled up beside her. His horse also was fretting, anxious to move on.

'Quite something, isn't it?' he said.

'It's incredible. So beautiful. You are so lucky to live here.'

'I know.' He paused for a moment, then said,

'After my father died and I came so close to losing it all, I realised then how much I loved it - the house, the land, everything. It's been worth the efforts of the last fifteen years putting it all back together.'

'And building a successful business at the same time. That's quite an achievement.'

'A means to an end. It was the only way I was going to make enough to restore the estate.'

But he's not happy, Kate thought. Despite his success, his wealth and his wonderful home. If only he could let go of the past and start living for the future, then he might find happiness.

'How do you feel?' he asked. 'Ready for a run?'

She nodded. 'Whenever you are.'

The horses needed no encouragement and broke straight into a canter. The wind in their faces, they kept pace with each other side by side.

It was intoxicating. Kate could barely resist shouting out loud. She wanted to whoop with joy. It was so good to be on a horse again, especially in such a magical place as this. She couldn't remember when she had enjoyed a ride as much.

She was well aware that it was partly because Ethan was there with her. Her whole body was acutely aware of his presence and she sensed that he was also enjoying being with her. She had felt his eyes on her as they'd climbed the combe, and knew he had been watching her, though he had tried to hide the fact. The thought that he might be finding her attractive, perhaps even a little disturbing, gave her a thrill of pleasure.

A gremlin inside her whispered, why not really give him something to look at?

No, she couldn't. Could she?

'Race you to that rock,' she called and, not giving him a chance to reply, she gave Bracken her head and galloped past him. She eased the reins and leant forward over the mare's neck lifting her weight from the saddle. The thunder of the horse's hooves matched the pounding of her heart as they flew across the springy turf. Just as she thought she was going to make it to the rock first, Ethan came up beside her and they arrived neck and neck.

'That was just amazing,' she called to him. 'And I almost beat you.'

Her cheeks were glowing and she was breathless with exhilaration. Was this real? Here she was, in this glorious place, riding a beautiful horse, in the company of an incredibly sexy man. What more could she want?

And, in that moment, she knew exactly what she wanted.

To be here with this man. This gorgeous man who made her heart thud and the very core of her being throb with desire.

To be here with Ethan.

Because she loved him.

The realisation stunned her and for a moment she couldn't think of a thing to say.

The two horses stood side by side, fidgeting,

tossing their heads, their hot breath like puffs of smoke in the cold air. Then Ethan's leg touched hers as the animals closed together, and she felt her pulse quicken at the contact.

'Just what was that in aid of?' he demanded.

For a second, she thought he was angry but the sparkle in his eyes betrayed him and she felt her confidence return.

'To prove to you that I can ride,' she retorted. 'And don't try and tell me you didn't enjoy it, too.'

§

And he had enjoyed it. Ethan couldn't remember when he had enjoyed himself more. Against his will, he was discovering that Kate was fun to be with. Far from helping him to forget her, this ride had made him even more conscious of her than before.

He had a horrible feeling she had been aware of him watching her. In fact he could swear she had been deliberately teasing him when she challenged him to that race and rode out in front of him. Did she know the effect the sight of those trousers, stretched tightly across her pert bottom as it hovered over the saddle, would have on him?

Yes. He was certain she did.

He'd hardly been able to keep his eyes off her since they'd left the stables. The way she rode, completely at ease with her mount. The shape of her legs as they gripped the mare's flanks. Her small hands, so light on the reins, every so often stroking Bracken's neck, encouraging her, steadying her as she picked her way up the hill path.

And now, her face glowed and her eyes shone. She was like a breath of fresh air. She seemed so open, so completely without guile. Perhaps he had been wrong about her. Wrong to assume she would be like all the other women he had been involved with who pretended affection but only wanted what his money would buy them.

He had a sudden urge to touch her, to put his arms round her, to feel her body against his. To hold her against him while he touched those laughing, parted lips with his own.

The horses stirred restlessly and again his leg brushed against Kate's. The sensation as they touched was like a fire shooting up his thigh, hot and demanding, re-igniting all the passion and desire that had been frozen within him for so long.

It was like a madness he couldn't control. Feelings, bottled up and denied for months, exploded into life.

Hardly aware of what he was doing, he leant towards her, seeing only her glowing face, her flashing green eyes, her soft lips which parted in welcome as he lowered his mouth to hers.

There was a moment of complete stillness as he savoured the taste of her and felt her respond to him. Then his horse sidled, eager to be off again, and they were dragged away from each other.

Neither of them spoke as if, by remaining

silent, the moment could be made to last for ever.

Then he saw her shiver and realised the evening was turning cold. The sun was beginning to thread subtle tendrils of red and gold through the blue-grey clouds and it wouldn't belong before it sank below the horizon. It was time they started back. The trees below them were already casting their shadows down the hill and it would be dusk before they made it home.

Reluctantly, his voice husky with desire, he said. 'Time we made a move. Okay?'

§

They rode back down the combe in silence. A silence so easy and companionable that, only a few hours ago, Kate couldn't have imagined it possible. She and Ethan had known each other for only a matter of days, and they seemed to have spent the whole of that time at loggerheads with each other.

Until he'd kissed her.

Her lips still burned from his touch. It had been so sudden, so unexpected, yet it was the very thing she'd been longing for. She re-lived the moment over and over in her mind as she followed him down the hill path. The moment he had leaned towards her and she had moved to meet him, drawn to him like a magnet, knowing exactly what he was going to do and wanting it with all of her being.

It was almost dark when they rode into the stable yard and dismounted.

Andy had finished his chores and gone home. The yard was quiet and deserted and the darkness of dusk closed around them, enveloping them a private world of their own.

They un-saddled the horses, rubbed them down, and fed and watered them without exchanging more than a few words. Almost, she thought, as if they were afraid they might break the spell and discover that, after all, nothing had changed; that they were still the same people as before and everything was as it always had been.

But she knew that was not the case. She was not the same person who had started off from here two hours ago. Then she had been free. Now, she was captive.

Before the kiss, she could have left Hanging Cross and gone back to Oxfordshire with only a bruised, but still repairable, heart. Now, she knew that everything she wanted in life was here, with this troubled, irascible man.

But it wouldn't be easy. Of that she was certain. His difficult manner hid the terrible hurt he was struggling to overcome. Maybe, this evening, he had taken the first faltering step towards healing that emotional damage. Maybe, if she was very careful, he would allow her to help him. Maybe she could even persuade him to go with her to the chapel.

Kate gave Bracken a final stroke and went out into the yard to wait for Ethan. While they had been inside the stables, the sun had finally set and the ink-black sky was alive with stars.

She moved over to the fence and leant backwards against the rails so that she could look up. She had never seen such a brilliant display. The Milky Way stretched like a rainbow of sequined smoke across the sky. She could see the Plough and Cassiopeia pointing across the sea to the Pole Star. In light-polluted London the stars had hardly ever been visible.

Footsteps crunched across the gravel and Ethan joined her, leaning back on the fence, hitching one heel backwards over the bottom rail.

She glanced towards him. 'It's so beautiful,' she whispered.

'One of the few places in the country where you get such a clear display.'

'And it's so quiet. We could be the only people in the whole universe.'

They were surrounded by blackness; the only light coming from the stars. An owl hooted and was answered by its mate. Muffled sounds drifted across to them from the loose boxes, of hooves in straw, the steady munching of hay and the occasional contented snicker of one of the horses.

So at peace was she, so completely captivated by the breathtaking spectacle above her that, when Ethan slipped his arm round her, it seemed perfectly natural and right to lean towards him. To let her head tilt sideways to rest against his shoulder. To relax into the warm strength of his arms. To breath in the scent of him.

She closed her eyes and sighed softly. This was where she wanted to be. Where she knew, instinctively, she belonged.

She felt his hand under her chin, lifting her face to his. Felt his fingers trace across her lips as she parted them in anticipation.

She opened her eyes and the look she surprised in his, set her heart thudding in her chest. Was it possible that he felt as she did? She hardly dared hope. But there was something in his expression she hadn't seen before, as if a small layer of defence had been peeled away, allowing her a brief glimpse of that part of him he took such great pains to hide from the world.

He smiled at her. Gently. Then he dropped a brief, tender kiss on her eager lips and said, softly. 'We must go in. Ruby will be serving dinner.'

Food was the last thing Kate felt like. She wanted to stay where she was, held in his arms, afraid that if they moved the spell would be broken and she would find that she had imagined it all.

Reluctantly, she followed him into the house and went up to her room in a state of suspended reality. She had never imagined it possible to feel so blissfully happy. Was this what it felt like to be high on drugs? This feeling of well-being; of anything being possible? This feeling of heightened awareness?

Slowly, she took off her clothes and stepped into the shower letting the warm water sluice down the length of her body, surrendering herself to the sensual feel of the water as it flowed across her breasts and stomach to fall in teasing, intimate rivulets along the inside of her thighs.

She wrapped her arms tightly round herself, revelling in the delicious sensation of loving and knowing she might be loved in return.

Almost as if sleep-walking, no longer tuned to the outside world but cocooned inside her own private heaven, she eventually towelled herself dry and dressed and made her way downstairs for dinner.

She could hardly keep her eyes off Ethan all through the meal. She could feel the electricity sparking between them each time their eyes met, as though they were linked by an invisible power line.

Surely Vanessa must be aware of the charged atmosphere? But, if she was, she made no sign.

§

Kate woke the following morning after a restless night. Her sleep had been filled with dreams, and several times she had woken, only to toss and turn as her mind and body re-lived that ride over the moor with Ethan.

She almost had to pinch herself to convince herself she wasn't still dreaming. That he really had kissed her. That she really did love him.

This was so different to what she had felt for Richard. Her feelings for him had been nothing but infatuation. Nothing compared with the feelings she had now for Ethan.

She lay back on the pillow and allowed her thoughts to free-wheel.

This was the last thing she had expected to happen. Ethan was older than her. He was richer than her. He came from an old land-owning family. He ran a multi-million-pound business that he had built up himself from scratch. How could she compete with that?

She was at least ten years his junior. Though not actually on the bread-line, she had always lived from day to day and had little in the way of savings. Her family were tenant farmers, scraping a living from agriculture at a time when many farmers were selling up, unable to make ends meet.

They could hardly be more different. Yet, the fact remained. She loved him.

Was there any chance that he might return her feelings?

Last night she had felt certain that he did but now, in the cold light of day, she doubted it. In fact, he was more likely to jump to the conclusion she was just after his money. The kiss had probably been just a spur of the moment reaction on his part to the exhilaration of the ride and the magic of their surroundings. She wouldn't be at all surprised if he was already regretting it.

If only he could find a way of getting over Caroline.

She wished there was some way she could

help him. If he could put that dreadful experience behind him, then he might be able to move on and open his heart to new relationships. But she knew it wouldn't be easy. So far he had shown little inclination to attempt it. He seemed to think that if he just closed his mind to the situation it would cease to exist.

She rolled over and hugged the pillow. What was she going to do?

It looked as though she had two choices. She could either stay here and resign herself to seeing him every day, loving him and wanting him, and all the time knowing that he was unattainable. Or she could leave now and go home and look for another job.

Neither option would do.

But there was a third. She could find a way to help him deal with his demons. There had to be something she could do.

She looked at the bedside clock. He would, no doubt, have been up for some time now. Would probably have been for his early-morning ride and be in his office, even though it was Sunday.

Vanessa didn't need her and she was free for the day but she couldn't imagine Ethan taking a day off.

Was he sitting at his desk, unable to concentrate on work for thinking of her? It was a lovely thought, but unlikely.

Was he efficiently closing his next deal and regretting his impulsive action? Much more likely.

Did he even remember the magic of yesterday evening?

There was only one way to find out.

She showered, and dressed in trousers and sweater. Perhaps he would let her take Bracken out on her own now that she seemed to have satisfied him she was a capable rider.

Then another idea occurred to her. Suppose she could tempt him to a walk down the cliff to the beach? Even, maybe, as far as the chapel? Did she dare suggest it?

She made her way downstairs. In the hall, she stopped by Jacob's portrait. Hands on hips, she studied his face. The hard planes and strong features were so like Ethan's. 'Oh, Jacob. What am I going to do?' she whispered.

She was the last one down to breakfast. Even the dogs had gone out.

'Gone for a walk with Miss Vanessa,' Ruby informed her.

'What about Ethan?'

'He came back from his ride about an hour ago. He's in his office.' She pointed to the coffee percolator on the Aga. 'I've made you some fresh coffee.'

Kate helped herself to a bowl of cereal and poured coffee. There was enough for several cups and it seemed a shame to waste it. She would take some to Ethan. Just the excuse she needed to go and see him.

Her pulse rate moved up a notch as she

knocked on the office door. What kind of mood would he be in? Would things still be the same as yesterday? Had that kiss really changed anything between them or had it just been a spontaneous reaction to the magic of the occasion?

'Yes?'

She swallowed. From his tone of voice it didn't look promising. He sounded short-tempered and irritable. Oh well. Faint heart never won and all that.

She pushed the door open and went in. He was sitting at his desk sorting through a pile of documents.

He looked up and their eyes met.

No. Nothing had changed. The air between them crackled like static. Her legs shook beneath her and her arms trembled.

'Perhaps you should put that down before you spill it all.' His voice broke the spell and she remembered the coffee she was holding. The mug was damp where the contents had spilled over onto the carpet.

'Damn.' Good start, Kate. Pull yourself together. 'I thought you might like some coffee,' she said.

'I'd love some. Thank you.'

She placed a mat on the corner of his desk and put the mug down. He must have been working for some time judging by the amount of paperwork in front of him. Then she noticed the file he had been studying.

It was the one she had dropped on the floor a couple of days ago when he had come into the office and accused her of prying into his private papers. The one she had gathered up in a temper and thrown down on the desk before walking out of the room.

The file marked Jacob's Chapel.

There was absolute silence. She was suddenly conscious that she was staring at the file and, worse, that Ethan knew that she had seen it.

Her heart was thumping so hard she could hear it. She could feel it beating in her chest, in her throat, in her head. She could barely breathe, she was so tense. Talk about bad timing. She could hardly have chosen a worse time to interrupt him.

How long had he been looking at it? And what had made him get it out now?

The silence dragged on. It could only have been a second or two but it felt like hours.

Which one of them was going to break it?

Her hand was still resting on the desk near the mug as if it had been frozen there.

She cleared her throat. 'I'm sorry,' she whispered. 'I … I think I'd better go.'

'No.' His hand shot out and grasped hers, preventing her from moving away. 'Don't go. That is, if you're not busy?'

'Er, no. Not busy at all. It's Sunday.' At that moment, it wouldn't have mattered how busy she was because she would gladly have thrown all to the wind in order to be here with him. 'Actually I came to see if you might like to ... ' her voice faded. She must be careful. One false step and she might lose all.

'I'd forgotten it was Sunday,' he said. 'What was it you had in mind?'

'Oh, nothing.' She shrugged it off. 'Nothing that won't wait.'

He gave her hand a squeeze before letting it go.

'Why don't you sit down?' He indicated the chair by his desk and she sank, gratefully, into it. The way her knees were wobbling, it wasn't a moment too soon. She wondered why he wanted her to stay. She could understand him wanting to work on a Sunday. He was that kind of a man. The sort that would always put work before play. But if he was working on the chapel file, surely he wouldn't want her to have anything to do with it? After the way he reacted the other time he found her looking at it, it must be the last thing he would want.

But maybe this was the opportunity she needed to broach the possibility of going there? She'd wait and see what he was going to say first before she said anything.

But he seemed to be having difficulty in finding the words.

He picked up his pen. Put the top on it. Laid it down on the desk. Straightened some papers. Leant back in his chair. Leant forward again and put his arms on the desk. Eventually he spoke.

'I think I owe you an apology.'

CHAPTER 8

T his was the last thing Kate expected. She opened her mouth to speak but he stopped her.

'No. Let me finish. I owe you an apology and I think I also owe you an explanation.'

Kate clasped her hands tightly together in her lap. Her palms were sweating with nervous anticipation and, though she couldn't have said quite why, she had a sense of being on the edge of a precipice. What was he going to say? Was he going to tell her more about Caroline? She hoped so. Talking about it all might help him to exorcise the painful memories.

She had a mental image of walking down the cliff path with Ethan, hand in hand, facing his past together, discussing it and obliterating it from his mind for ever so that he could be free to love again.

His face betrayed the struggle he was having finding the right words but, at last he spoke.

'I hardly know where to begin.' His voice was low and tight with tension. He cleared his throat. 'Firstly, I have to apologise for the way I've treated you since you arrived. I guess I've made things pretty difficult for you.'

That's putting it mildly. The words flashed through Kate's head but she kept silent. Said nothing.

'There is a reason for that, but I'm afraid it's not something I can talk about.' He paused and then added, so quietly that she almost missed the words, ' I wish I could.'

Then, his voice stronger, he said, 'As you will have guessed, I once had plans to convert the chapel into living accommodation. I had thought it would make a holiday cottage. Actually, to be more exact, I pictured it as a honeymoon cottage. No,' he shook his head, reading Kate's mind as she immediately leapt to the wrong conclusion, 'not for myself. The idea was to create something very special that could be marketed specifically to honeymoon couples.'

He gave a wry smile. 'You have to admit that it is a very romantic setting.'

'Oh, yes. I think it's a wonderful idea. It's so secluded, no-one would know they were there and they'd have complete privacy. I can't imagine anything more romantic.'

'We were almost ready to go ahead, plans drawn up, permission granted for change of use, everything. Hence this file.' He waved his arm across the papers spread on the desk. 'It was all set to begin when …. when Caroline and I returned from our own honeymoon. It was when I went down to check some measurements that I found them.'

§

Ethan paused as the memory of that discovery gripped and twisted at his guts. The expression on Kate's face was almost his undoing. She was looking at him as if she was living it with him. He'd been afraid she would pity him or, even worse, think him a fool. But she seemed to understand.

He had kept it all buried inside him for so long that the relief at finally being able to talk to someone about it was almost overwhelming.

How many nights, how many months, had he lain in bed unable to sleep while the memories and the images seared through his mind?

Even now, the picture was cuttingly sharp. In his mind he could see the chapel as he'd walked into it, expecting it to be deserted as usual. The late afternoon sun was weak and the interior was dark. A rustle had startled him and, thrusting the door wide open, he'd snapped on his torch and swung the beam round in the direction of the sound.

The building had been used as a store for various pieces of old furniture and the pair had made excellent use of it.

The words spilled out as he emptied his soul to Kate.

'All she wanted was money. That had been their plan all along. The affair had been going on for months. Even before I met her. Can you imagine that? Can you imagine anyone being that mercenary?'

Then he noticed Kate's face. Her bottom lip was caught in her teeth and her eyes were misted. My God, she wasn't going to cry, was she? If she did, he had a horrible feeling he might join her. He looked away quickly and picked up his pen. He needed something to fiddle with. Something to do with his hands. He looked down, deliberately keeping his eyes off her.

'That's why the project was cancelled. A honeymoon cottage. Hah! How ironic is that? I haven't been near the place since. Haven't wanted anything to do with it. That's why I was so angry when I saw you looking at this file. This morning I was going to take the whole damn lot to the shredder and forget it ever existed. Unfortunately I can't so easily get rid of the building.'

At last, he looked at her again. Why was he talking to her like this? What was it about her that made him want to tell her everything, to share his pain with her and have her smooth it away? He'd spent most of the night re-living that kiss and the feel of his arm around her as they gazed up at the stars. Then he had slept, only to dream of doing it again. Only, in his dreams, it hadn't stopped at just a kiss.

'I don't know why I'm telling you all this.'

He threw the pen down. It wasn't helping. He pushed back from the desk. He needed to move. Needed action to calm his nerves. He got to his feet.

'God damn it, we've known each other less than a week and I'm saying things to you that I've never said to anyone before.'

§

Kate longed to be able to reach out to him; to run her fingers across the taut muscles of his face, and smooth away the hurt she saw there. Her heart wept for him. What must it have been like for him to find the woman he loved in the arms of another man? To know his wife had been sleeping with someone else even through the months of their courtship and marriage? And to know she had only been interested in his wealth.

Cautiously, she stood and leant across the desk and rested her hand on his arm.

'Ethan,' she whispered. 'You have to find a way of dealing with this.

'He jerked his arm away, raising both hands to rake his hair. His brow furrowed with despair. 'Do you think I haven't tried?' His voice was ragged with the effort of controlling it.

'But you go out of your way to avoid thinking of it.'

'And why do you think that might be?' he snapped.

She recoiled at the ferocity in his voice. She opened her mouth to speak but he didn't pause.

'Do you think I want to be reminded of how she made a bloody fool of me? Took me in so completely? What's the word they used to use? Cuckold, wasn't it? Well that's what she made of me. And you want me to think about it?'

He punched both hands onto the desk, leaning against it for support, head bowed, teeth clenched.

Kate moved round the desk to stand beside him. The urge to touch him was irresistible. She reached up and smoothed down the mess of hair where his fingers had ploughed through. The pain in his eyes was almost more than she could bear. She slid her fingers gently down the side of his face, over the hard planes of his cheekbones, willing the tense muscles to relax.

There was a moment of stillness, then, without warning, he stood and grabbed her hand, pressing it hard to his face as if drawing strength from her touch. For long seconds he stood, eyes closed, his breath rasping as he fought to control his anguish.

Then his eyes opened and sought hers and held them as he, oh so slowly, drew her hand down from his cheek, across his chin, and brought her palm to rest against his mouth. His breath was warm against her skin and she could feel the softness of his lips on the sensitive centre of her hand.

Her breath caught in her throat and she swallowed. In that moment she knew she wanted him. All of him. This was what she had been longing for, without any real hope it might ever happen. Might there be a chance for them after all?

Don't stop at my hand. For a moment she was afraid she had spoken aloud.

As if he'd heard, he released her trembling palm and placed his hands each side of her face. She shivered as his spread fingers slid over the skin of her temples to bury themselves in her hair. His thumbs played gently over the sensitive area beneath her eyes.

She was floating, as if her body no longer had any substance. She was drowning in exquisite sensuousness.

'Kate.' His warm breath sighed across her ear as he murmured her name.

Then his mouth was on hers, swelling her lips with its urgency. His tongue teased its way on to hers. His hands moved to the back of her head pressing her closer so she could hardly breathe, and her own hands responded, pulling his head down to her own. They clung to each other, locked in mutual desire.

God, how she loved this man. This bitter, disillusioned, bad-tempered, gorgeous man who needed her help to conquer his demons. And she knew, without a doubt, that she would do anything in her power to help him.

Eventually, Ethan lifted his mouth from hers and dropped his hands to her shoulders. He slid them slowly down her arms until he could take her hands in his. Then he backed towards the desk, keeping hold of her so that, arms outstretched, she had no choice but to follow him.

He perched on the edge of the desk and pulled her closer until she was standing between his parted knees. Her body tingled with expectation. He pulled her closer still. His hands loosed hers and slipped round her waist until she could feel the pressure of them in the small of her back and she shivered as he traced the ridge of her spine down to its very tip. He made her feel naked, as if he could see every curve, every crease of her body. And she revelled in it.

He pulled her closer until their bodies touched. She could feel his arousal and her own body pulsed in response. He kissed her neck just below her ear then, lightly, tantalisingly, he kissed his way along the underneath of her jaw bone, down over her throat, and across her collar bone, nosing the edge of her shirt out of the way as he went.

With a grunt of frustration, he slid his left hand further round her hips to maintain his hold on her and raised his right hand to the buttons that were impeding his progress. Kate caught her breath as, one by one, he unfastened them. His fingers began to explore the valley between her breasts, dipping teasingly under the edge of her bra. Was it possible to die of desire? Her body screamed for satisfaction.

'Ethan.' She groaned his name.

Then wished she hadn't.

The sound of her voice seemed to bring Ethan to his senses. His mouth lifted from hers. His fingers stilled. He hugged her to him for a moment then dropped a tender kiss on her forehead and stepped back.

His voice was raw as he spoke. 'I'm sorry. I never intended that to happen.'

Kate struggled to think straight, her senses still in overdrive. Something had to give and before she knew it, the words were out.

'Why ever not? You've wanted to for long enough?'

His head snapped up.

'In case you'd forgotten, I'm still married.'

'And you'll soon be divorced.'

His voice was ice-cold as he replied. 'Yes; because my wife took a lover. I have no intention of lowering myself to her level.'

Kate turned her back and concentrated on fastening her buttons. Tears pricked her eyes and she blinked them back. Why on earth had she said that? She'd probably undone all the progress she'd made over the past few days. She had so much wanted to persuade him to go to the chapel and face whatever demons he found there. She was so certain that, if only he would do that, he could begin to love again.

It had been a mistake to touch him. If she hadn't reached out and touched his arm, probably none of this would have happened. Would it be possible to repair the damage?

She fastened the last of the buttons and braced herself to turn round. He must still be in the room. She hadn't heard him leave. She took a deep calming breath and …

'I'm sorry.' His voice was close. She could sense him standing behind her. She turned to face him.

His hands were thrust into his trouser pockets. It gave her a momentary satisfaction to think that perhaps he couldn't trust himself to let them out. He looked almost sheepish as he spoke.

'That was unforgivable of me.' His spread his hands in a gesture of puzzlement before pushing them back in his pockets. 'I didn't mean to suggest that you are …'

Satisfying though it was to see his discomfort, Kate decided to help him out. Maybe she hadn't lost too much ground after all.

She smiled and held out a hand. 'I'm sorry, too. I shouldn't have said what I did. How about we forgive each other and start again?'

He squeezed her hand. 'Sounds like a good idea. So, do we carry on from here? Or do we forget any of this happened?'

'As I'm not sure either of us could forget, I suggest we go from here.'

'Which reminds me. I think you were about to suggest going somewhere before we got … er … sidetracked?'

This was the opening she needed but was it the right moment? It could turn out to be disastrous. On the other hand it could be the only chance she was going to get. Perhaps this was one time when she shouldn't think too hard before speaking?

'Okay. But I'm not sure you're going to like it.'

She paused, steeling herself for his reaction.

He raised an eyebrow. 'I'm intrigued.'

It was now or never.

'I was going to ask you if you would come to the chapel with me.'

§

It was the last thing Ethan had expected.

He knew perfectly well why Kate was suggesting it. He knew, himself, that he would never completely lay the ghost of Caroline and all that had happened until he could face up to it. One day he must go there.

The memory of the time he discovered her, every detail, every action, every sound, was hot branded into his brain. When he thought of it, he could still feel the reactions of his own body as if it was yesterday. The shock, the disbelief. The adrenalin rush sending the blood hammering through his head so he couldn't think straight.

They hadn't heard him come in until he slammed the door back on its hinges. He'd swung the torch violently trapping the two figures in the beam, galvanising them into action. He'd heard Caroline's sharp intake of breath as she realised what was happening. Saw her lover grab his clothes and make a run for it. Swung the heavy torch at him - but missed. If he'd been able to lay his hands on him he would have killed him.

Caroline was made of sterner stuff. After her initial shock, she had calmly pulled a cover over her naked body and sat there, smiling up at him, knowing he could never have brought himself to harm her.

But the damage was done. In that moment his love for her had died to be replaced with a cold loathing.

She'd agreed so readily to his demand for a divorce that he was certain she had planned it from the beginning. All she wanted was a large settlement, to which he had consented, because the alternative - having it dragged through the courts - would have been too humiliating. And he knew without a doubt that Caroline would have had no compunction whatever about making all the shameful details public knowledge.

Until Kate, no woman had managed to penetrate the defences he'd erected to protect the soft centre that still clung to life somewhere deep inside him. If only she didn't … he couldn't bring himself to even think the words for fear they might release a monster. He knew he ought to tell her but it was too soon. He would. Sometime. If everything worked out.

She was waiting for his reply.

And he did not want to go.

But, he owed her. He had almost given in to his physical need for her and, if she hadn't spoken his name when she had, he knew he would have taken her right here in the office. The fact that she clearly wanted him to made no difference. When, if, they made love, it would be in the right place at the right time.

§

Kate held her breath and waited, watching the changing emotions reflected in his face. Was the fact that he hadn't immediately refused, a good sign? She allowed herself to hope.

The he turned to look at her and smiled. 'You do know you are probably the only person who could persuade me to do this?'

She felt her heart flip as he held out his hand to her and said, 'Let's go fight the demons.'

It was a beautiful day. The sun shone warm on their faces as they made their way down the cliff path. The ground had dried out and the stone steps under their feet were no longer slippery. The whole atmosphere felt friendly and welcoming and Kate felt a surge of optimism as she followed Ethan down the slope, the narrowness of the path preventing them from walking side by side. The air was so still. There was hardly a sound. Everywhere was quiet and peaceful.

They stepped onto the beach and the silence was broken by the rattle and scrape of the large stones beneath their feet as they crunched across them towards the scalloped edge of the incoming water.

There, they stood for a moment, allowing the silence to recover, enjoying the view and each other's company, neither of them speaking.

There was no wind. Hardly any movement at

all. The surface of the sea was so calm it looked like a sheet of pale blue ice, streaked here and there with the darker blues of strong underwater currents. The waves were barely waves at all, just gentle ripples that lapped across the shingle with scarcely a whisper.

The silence was momentarily broken by the aerial warbling of a skylark. Kate watched it soaring and hovering as it sang, and sighed with contentment. This place was so beautiful. So peaceful. Such a contrast to London where there was no escape from the constant intrusive noise of traffic and people. Who needed exotic resorts and tropical islands when there was such beauty right here at home?

She breathed deeply, drinking in the splendour of the vast curving bay surrounded by its horseshoe of protective hills. Sunshine illuminated the far headlands where the steep coastal cliffs dipped down to the sea.

Then above them, a bird called, a different sound this time, and Ethan caught her arm and pointed upwards.

'Look,' he breathed. 'A Hen Harrier. Isn't it beautiful? They're still a rare sight round here.' He smiled at her. 'You're honoured.'

Kate watched, fascinated, as the bird circled lazily in the sky before raising its black-tipped wings and gliding down to swoop on its prey, somewhere out of their sight on the heather-clad hill. It was a magic moment.

They were alone on the beach. Ethan's hand was still resting on her arm and they were standing so close she could feel the chemistry working between them. They might have been one person, so in tune did she feel with him and with their surroundings. A faint breeze came from nowhere and teased her hair. Her blood pulsed to the calm, rippling rhythm of the sea. She lowered her gaze from the sky at the same moment that Ethan did, and their faces turned towards each other. Their eyes met. His lips hovered above hers. She closed her eyes and willed him to kiss her.

There was a sudden rush of sound and …

'Aaah.' She yelped and jumped as a rogue wave washed round their legs, and they fell against each other and dissolved into laughter.

'Darn it,' she groaned. 'Now I'm soaked.'

He placed his hands on her shoulders and held her at arms length. 'You'll soon dry out.'

His eyes were sparkling with humour and, for the first time, she noticed little creases of laughter lines. He looked relaxed and happy which, considering their objective, was the last thing she would have expected.

He gave her a playful tug. 'Come on. A drop of water won't do you any harm. Let's go.'

'You're a heartless beast,' she teased him as they squelched away from the incoming tide.

'You won't notice the wet if you keep walking and keep your feet warm.'

Maybe he was right. Thank goodness she was

wearing deck shoes and not her good boots.

As they left the beach and turned in amongst the trees, the sun became shaded and the air cooled. Sunlight still filtered through, catching the tips of the leaves as they moved in the breeze but Kate was conscious of a subtle change in the atmosphere. Was it because of the shade? Or was it a change in within themselves?

They stopped in front of the chapel. She had expected it to be dark and gloomy but she saw that the sun had moved round and was shining in from behind the building, its rays penetrating the dirty glass windows. Inside it would be sun-lit. Brighter, more cheerful, than it had been when she came here on her own two days ago.

She longed to reach out to Ethan and take his hand, to help him, but sensed he wouldn't want her to. She heard him sigh and take a deep breath as if trying to draw courage from his surroundings.

Then he turned to her. His expression was blank, as though he had deliberately purged himself of all emotion. His voice was tight, brittle, as he spoke.

'I have to do this alone, Kate. Will you wait for me outside?'

Kate nodded and smiled. 'I'll be on the beach.'

§

Ethan stepped through the door and into the past.

There was no sound apart from a gentle

fluttering where the breeze played through the ivy that threaded between the gaps in the windows. On one side of the chapel, dust motes danced in the bright sunlight. On the other, all was shadows and dark corners.

He sat down on one of the few surviving pews. It was a small building and had probably rarely been used for its professed intended purpose. Indeed, he doubted it had ever been consecrated.

From what he had been able to learn of Jacob, he could not imagine him as a church-goer and it was more than likely he had built the chapel purely as a secure hiding place for contraband goods. As a place of worship, it would have been relatively safe from the attention of the excise men.

Was it such a short time ago that he had walked in here and found Caroline?

He had left the place as it was that day, having no wish to return. The old stored furniture remained in an untidy pile against the opposite wall.

The couch still stood to one side, silent witness to her infidelity and betrayal. He stared at it, remembering the events of that day, waiting for the pain to begin, for the memories to flood back and tear at his heart.

But it didn't happen.

He had expected to feel anger; despair; hurt. But he felt none of those things. Instead, he felt utterly devoid of all emotion … except, perhaps, relief.

§

Kate found a large flat pebble near the top of the beach away from the encroaching tide and sat on it.

She tried to concentrate on the view but her thoughts persisted in returning to Ethan and wondering how he was feeling. She knew this was going to be make or break and prayed she had done the right thing in persuading him to come down here.

If it worked out as she hoped, there might be a future for them. If it didn't, she might as well pack her bags and go home because there was no way she could remain at Hanging Cross and maintain a platonic relationship with Ethan.

She sat, lost in her thoughts, unaware of the passing of time, until a widening strip of wet shingle in front of her, made her realise that the tide had turned and the sea was gradually retreating down the beach.

She shuffled uneasily on her hard stone seat. What was keeping Ethan? What kind of mood would he be in? She wished he would hurry up and come back so they could get it over with. At least then she would know, one way or another.

And then, of course, there was that other little matter that had been puzzling her right from the beginning. What wouldn't she give to know the answer to that?

There was a scrunch of pebbles and she looked

up to see Ethan walking towards her. She screwed up her eyes, trying to make out the expression on his face but he kept his head down as if deep in thought.

She stayed where she was, sitting with her legs drawn up, arms around her knees, holding her breath in anticipation.

He stood for a moment in front of her, his legs spread, hands thrust into his jacket pockets, not speaking. She waited. Was he going to say anything? What was he thinking?

Then he smiled and dropped down beside her on the shingle.

Not daring to speak, she raised her eyebrows in query, waiting for him to speak first. Then she breathed a sigh of relief when he said, 'You were right. I should have done this long ago. I went inside and I felt nothing. Absolutely nothing. It was just a dingy building, full of dust and cobwebs, bits of furniture and some old memories.'

He reached out and took her hand in his. 'I don't suppose,' he went on, 'I'll ever completely forget what happened there but I know now it has lost its power to hurt. What I feel most is anger. No …' He raised a hand to stop her as she began to interrupt. '…not anger at them. Anger at myself for allowing it to mess up my life for so long. It's time I put it behind me.'

Kate closed her eyes and allowed herself to relax. In that moment she realised how tense she had been, how much she had been dreading the possible outcome. It could all have gone so wrong. That it hadn't was nothing short of a miracle and the relief was overwhelming.

Impetuously, she flung her arms round his neck and kissed his cheek. 'Oh, Ethan, I'm so glad.'

His reaction was immediate. He turned his head towards her and Kate felt her heart flip at the feel of his skin moving across her lips. Then his mouth met hers and she could taste the salt of the sea air. He lifted his hands to caress her cheeks, stroke her temples. Then he buried his fingers in her hair and the pressure on her mouth increased as he pulled her towards him. He eased his tongue between her lips, found her own tongue, dipped and teased until she thought she could bear it no longer.

She moaned as desire fired through her, pulsing along her thighs and throbbing deep into her belly. Her body was crying out for him.

Then the pressure on her mouth ceased and she felt Ethan's breath whisper across her face as he spoke.

'Kate …?'

'Mmm?'

'Kate, listen to me.'

She gave a little murmur of protest as he lifted his head and gathered her into his arms, pulling her into him so that she leant against him, her head resting on his shoulder. She sighed with contentment. Being in his arms felt so good, so right. This was where she wanted to be always, here with this man who she loved so very much. She snuggled herself into a more comfortable position. His head rested on hers and she could feel her hair stirring slightly as he breathed.

'Kate.' His voice was quiet. 'I've decided to go ahead with the conversion into a dwelling.'

Surprised, she looked up at him. 'You have?'

'I have.'

'Oh, that's wonderful.' She was thrilled.

'I just hope it isn't jinxed as a honeymoon cottage.'

'You mean, will it have bad vibes? Will ghosts of the past come back to haunt it?'

He gave a chuckle. 'It does sound a bit melodramatic, doesn't it.'

'I should think, if anything, it would help to exorcise the place.'

He put his hand under her chin and tilted her head back so that their eyes met. 'I think you have already done that,' he said, quietly.

How long they stayed there, Kate wasn't sure but it was getting late by the time they started back along the beach. She was hungry and realised it must be long past lunch. But what did it matter? It had been a wonderful morning; far more successful than she had ever imagined possible. She hardly dared hope that Ethan felt towards her as she did towards him but she could wait. Give it time and who knew what might happen. He had crossed a major hurdle. Maybe now they could both move on from here.

CHAPTER 9

'But that's wonderful news!' Vanessa beamed as she threw her arms around Ethan and hugged him.

Kate smiled to herself as she watched Ethan squirm with embarrassment at his aunt's enthusiastic reaction. He finally extracted himself from her embrace and, giving her a quick kiss on her cheek, moved to the opposite side of the kitchen table.

'The first thing will be to get the access road repaired so that we can get vehicles down there,' he said. 'Kate has offered to help out with the admin if you can continue to spare her, Nessa.'

'Of course I can, but,' she turned to Kate, 'are you sure you want to, Kate? It will be a lot of extra work on top of what you do for me?'

Kate nodded. 'I'm sure. I'm as excited by the project as everyone else. I shall enjoy taking part in it.'

'Well, if you're certain, it's fine by me. When do you plan to begin, Ethan?'

'I'll speak to Harry first thing tomorrow and

then I'll drive down there and take a good look. Do you want to come, Kate?'

'Just try stopping me.'

'Can you be ready by eight?'

'Any time to suit you.'

'Good. I'll have her back by lunch time, Nessa, so you won't lose out on her time with you.'

Vanessa flapped her hands dismissively. 'Oh, I know Kate won't let me down. I'm just so thrilled you are going ahead with it.'

'Yes, well,' Ethan was beginning to look decidedly uncomfortable. 'I have some things to do in the office if I'm to be ready for the morning so, if you'll excuse me, I shall see you both at dinner.'

Kate glanced at him as he strode past and she felt her face grow warm as, with his back to his aunt, he grinned and gave her a conspiratorial wink, sending shivers of pleasure rippling down her spine.

'My dear,' Vanessa said when he had gone, 'I'm dying to know what changed his mind but, perhaps I shouldn't ask?'

Kate recalled the events of the day and felt her cheeks grow warm. 'I'd rather you didn't,' she murmured.

'Don't worry. I won't embarrass you. All I can say is that you have somehow wrought a miracle and for that you have my eternal gratitude. I had almost given up hope. Let's pray that all goes well from now on.'

§

The Land Rover lurched and jolted and Ethan cursed as he fought to control the steering wheel as it threatened to wrench itself from his hands. It was his own fault for neglecting the road for so long and now he was paying the price.

Winter floods had carried soil and stones down from the moor and from the surrounding farmland, coating the road surface with a layer of debris. Winter frosts had opened up pot holes which the floodwater had filled and scoured and which now rendered the road barely passable.

He stole a sideways glance at Kate in the passenger seat. She was hanging on with both hands but, he was relieved to see, looking as though she was thoroughly enjoying herself. He hit a pothole and felt the jar in his arms as the steering wheel pulled to one side.

'Are you okay?' he asked, seeing Kate's seatbelt tighten round her as the jolt almost threw her from her seat.

She grinned. 'I'm fine.'

'If I'd known it was this bad, I wouldn't have asked you to come with me.'

'I wouldn't have missed it for anything. Ouch!' She grimaced as they hit another pothole.

'Sorry. I should never have let it get so bad. It's difficult to believe this amount of damage could be done in such a short time.'

They had followed the single-track road from

its junction with the main coast road, dropping steeply almost to sea-level before winding through trees, bracken and gorse until it reached the chapel, a few yards from the beach. When Ethan pulled up outside the chapel, Harry Crawford was waiting for them, his own Land Rover parked in front.

He came forward to greet them.

'Ethan, good morning. Hello, Kate.'

Ethan nodded to him. 'Harry. Glad to see you made it okay. It looks as though we have some serious work to do on the road. That's obviously the first priority so I want the contractors onto it as soon as possible.'

Harry nodded. 'Right.'

'Let's get inside and go over the plans.'

He took Kate's arm and led her through the door into the dim interior. It seemed strange being here with her after all that had happened. Memories lurked in every corner but they were old ones and no longer had the power to hurt. Carrying on with this project would enable him to throw out the memories along with the rubbish, cleanse the building, and cleanse the place deep inside himself where the memories had festered for too long.

He spread the plans out on the stone slab that had served Jacob as an altar. Whatever else this building had been used for over its long life, he was pretty sure it had never been used for any religious purpose. He had never been able to find any records to show it had ever been consecrated.

Kate had wandered off to look round while he and Crawford discussed the work to be done. Eventually, he left Crawford to check measurements and went to join her.

He put an arm round her shoulders and dropped a kiss on her neck. 'Come with me.'

He led her through an archway in the north wall and into the room he had always thought of as the vestry, though it was more likely to have stored contraband than any vestments.

'This will be the bedroom. The window faces east so will get the morning sun.'

'It's lovely. I can just imagine waking in here with the sun streaming through the window.' She moved against him and laid her head on his shoulder. 'Then, eventually, strolling down to the sea for a swim …'

'Eventually?' He interrupted her with a grin.

She gave him a sideways look. 'Well, it is for honeymoon couples.'

He laughed and hugged her. He couldn't remember when he had felt so light-hearted.

They went back into the main body of the chapel.

'This alcove here,' he said, 'will be partitioned off to make a bathroom and kitchen and the rest of the space will be living area. What do you think?'

'I think it will be perfect.'

§

Kate was eating breakfast the following morning when Ethan entered the kitchen carrying a travelling bag and his briefcase. He was dressed casually in chinos and cotton shirt, but carrying his dark grey business suit on a hanger over his shoulder.

'You look as though you're going somewhere,' Kate commented between spoonfuls of muesli.

The atmosphere between them was so different now. It was difficult to believe they were the same people. Ethan was so much more relaxed, so much more at ease with her - and with himself.

'Something's come up, I'm afraid. I had a call from the office early this morning which means I have to go up to London for a few days.' He put his luggage down and sat at the table next to her. 'It's the last thing I wanted just now but it can't be helped. I don't know how long I'll be away but it shouldn't be for too long. I wanted a quick word with you about what we discussed yesterday.'

'The renovation of the chapel?'

'Yes. I've spoken to Harry Crawford. He's going to start things moving with the contractors. I hate leaving you to hold the fort on your own but I promise I will sort something out about a temp to help you when I get back. Are you sure you will be able to manage?'

'Of course I will. I'm looking forward to it.' Kate felt a glow of satisfaction spread through her at the prospect of beginning the project. Ethan was a changed man. She was seeing a side of him that she hadn't seen before. He was positive and cheerful. And he was friendly. That was the best part of it. He was actually being friendly towards her. She also felt absurdly pleased that he felt he could trust her to keep an eye on things while he was away.

'I've left all the relevant papers on the desk. I think everything's there but if I've missed anything it'll be in the filing cabinet or one of the desk drawers. You know your way round the office now, so feel free to look for anything you need.'

He looked at his watch and stood up. 'I'll have to go. Sorry to be so brief but,' he handed her a card, 'these are my contact details, and Crawford will know where to get hold of me as well.'

He reached to Kate and pulled her to her feet - just as the phone began to ring.

'Darn it. Let's hope that's nothing urgent. I really do need to be on my way.'

They both turned as Ruby came into the kitchen.

'Telephone message for you,' she said.

Ethan sighed. 'Who is it Ruby?'

'Not for you, sir. It's for Kate.

'For me?' Kate was taken aback. Who on earth would be phoning her on the house number? Her family and friends all used her mobile.

'He said to tell you,' Ruby said, 'that Richard rang and he'll call you back later.'

Kate felt the colour drain from her face and her limbs begin to tremble. She reached for the chair she had just vacated, and sat down again. What did Richard think he was playing at? Would he never leave her alone? She glanced at Ethan and was dismayed at the expression on his face.

'Thank you, Ruby,' he said, dismissively. He waited for Ruby to leave the room and turned to Kate.

'What's all this about?'

'I don't know.'

'I thought you told me that you were finished with him? That it was all over and done with?'

'I am. It is.' Impatiently, Kate stood up again, scraping the chair across the flagstone floor.

Ethan grabbed her arm and turned her towards him. 'Then why is he phoning you?'

Kate shrugged off his hand and began to pace across the floor. 'I honestly don't know. Believe me, I have no idea what he is up to.'

'Ex boyfriends don't just telephone out of the blue. You must have given him some encouragement.'

'I haven't. Just the opposite in fact.'

Oh, why hadn't she told Ethan about Richard's persistent phone calls earlier? Not only might he have been able to help her, but then this situation wouldn't have arisen. It must look to Ethan as though she had been carrying on behind his back. She stopped pacing and stood with her back to the Aga, arms folded across her chest, trying to steady her nerves.

'Ethan,' she said, fighting to control the shake

in her voice, 'listen to me. Please. Richard has been texting and phoning me ever since I arrived here. I have tried to stop him but he just won't take no for an answer.'

Ethan didn't speak but his expression was grim. The barriers were up again. Was she going to be able to break through? He was standing, legs apart, hands thrust into his pockets, watching her, his eyes no more than slits, his mouth a hard set line.

She carried on. 'When I left London, as far as I was concerned we were finished. I never wanted to see him again and I told him so. I thought that would be the end of it. But the first night I was here, he tried to ring me. I sent him a message telling him to leave me alone. I couldn't have made it clearer that I wanted nothing more to do with him but for some reason he's been pestering me ever since.'

She paused, hoping for some sort of response from Ethan. When none came, she went towards him, holding out her arms, hoping he would take her hands.

But he kept his hands in his pockets. His attitude was as cold as his voice. 'Why didn't you say something? I could have dealt with him for you.'

'I so nearly did but ...'

He cut her short. 'Perhaps you didn't want to be rid of him? Perhaps you enjoyed having two men at the same time? You wouldn't be the only woman to feel that way.'

'Ethan!' Her voice was a wail of disbelief. 'How could you think that of me? After everything we've been through? I thought you trusted me.'

'Well that shows how wrong you can be about someone. Trust has to be earned.'

She couldn't believe she was hearing this. 'How dare you say that to me,' she snapped, her temper rising.

'Trust goes both ways. You clearly didn't trust me enough to tell me about the calls.'

I wanted to tell you but I was afraid to in case you reacted exactly as you are doing.'

He made a gesture of dismissal and began to collect his things.

Kate felt panic rising. She couldn't let him go off to London with this hanging unresolved between them. Think, Kate. Think. There must be some way of convincing him she was telling the truth. He was moving towards the door.

'Wait.' The word came out louder than she meant it to. A desperate appeal for his attention. 'Wait. I can prove it.'

He hesitated. Stood in the doorway, waiting.

Kate looked around her, searching frantically for the jacket she'd brought down with her that morning. She dragged it from the back of the chair and reached into the pocket. She pulled out her mobile and moved towards Ethan, punching keys as she went.

They were still there. All the messages from

Richard, together with her replies. She had meant to delete them but, thank goodness, had never got round to it.

She thrust the phone towards Ethan.

'Look,' she told him.

Slowly, he took the phone from her and looked down the list of calls.

'Now do you believe me?'

For a moment, he said nothing. Then he put his arms around her and laid his head on hers.

When he spoke, his voice was muffled.

'I'm sorry. Can you forgive me?'

She hugged him to her. 'Please believe me, Ethan. I would never do anything like that. You are the only man I want. The only one I will ever want. Don't you realise that I love you?'

There. She'd said it.

He stood back and tilted her chin so that their eyes met. He looked at her for long moments then, his voice so low and husky she almost melted, he said, 'I love you, too.'

Kate shivered as he lowered his head and their lips met. His kiss was tender, gentle. Unlike his previous passionate embraces. Seconds passed.

Then Ethan pulled away. 'I have to go. I wish I didn't, but I'm afraid I must. I'm going to be late as it is. And don't worry. We will deal with this matter when I get back.'

He collected his bags and made for the door. Then he stopped and came back to her and dropped a kiss on her forehead. 'Take care,' he said.

'See you in a few days.'

Kate followed him and stood in the porch, waving, as he drove out of the yard, through the gate, and disappeared up the hill.

The house suddenly seemed empty without him.

She spent the first part of the morning in the estate office dealing with the post and some letters he had left for her to answer. She searched out some papers for Harry Crawford. Then, not having anything else to do there, she decided to make an early start with Vanessa's work. The writing was going well and Kate was kept busy most of the afternoon typing up the latest chapters. She took the dogs out for a walk after dinner and decided to have an early night.

Not only did the house feel empty without Ethan. She felt empty - as if she'd lost a vital part of herself. She missed him so much. Did he feel the same, she wondered. Was he missing her? Wishing he was with her at Hanging Cross instead of in London? Somehow she doubted it. He was not the kind of man to allow personal matters to affect his business and would have his mind fixed firmly on his work.

She slept fitfully, dreaming of shipwrecks, secret lovers, and of Ethan, dressed as a smuggler and looking for all the world like Jacob Cade.

The next few days passed slowly even though she was extra busy coping with Ethan's office work as well as typing for Vanessa every afternoon.

Most mornings, she woke early and, knowing she was likely to have a busy day, had early breakfast before going to the estate office and making a start on Ethan's post.

Ethan had been gone four days and it felt more like four weeks. She opened the post as usual and sorted out the letters that needed a reply before drafting a brief response to each stating that Ethan would be in touch on his return. She hoped he would be back soon. Not because of the work but because she was missing him so much. The office and the house felt empty without him and she was realising what a strong personality he had.

She was typing up the final letter when the phone rang.

It was Harry Crawford.

'Kate, I'm down at the chapel. I have to take some measurements and make a few final checks. I could do with someone to take notes and I wondered if you were free?'

It would be good to get out of the office for a while, especially if it meant a walk down to the beach.

'I can be ready in about twenty minutes if that's alright?'

'That's fine. There's a file I need you to bring with you if you can find it. It'll save me having to come up to the house.'

'Sure. Which one?'

'It's a green one, labelled 'Preliminary Drawings'. It'll probably be in the filing cabinet.'

'Okay.'

'Thanks. The only thing is, the road isn't quite finished yet and it probably wouldn't be wise to drive your car along it. I'd come and fetch you but I'm with the contractor.'

'That's okay. I'll come down the cliff path. I shall enjoy the walk. See you soon.'

Kate quickly completed the letters and put them ready for the post then went to find the file Harry wanted. She searched the drawer where she knew it ought to be, but without success. Then she remembered Ethan had had the files for the chapel out on his desk a couple of days ago. Perhaps he had put it somewhere else. She was reluctant to search his desk - it seemed too private - but he had told her to feel free to look if she needed to. She pulled out the drawers, one at a time. In the large bottom drawer she found what she was looking for among a pile of other files and papers.

She glanced at her watch. It had taken longer than she had anticipated. Harry would be waiting for her and she still had to get changed. Quickly, she pulled the file from the drawer and shoved it into her bag then she rushed quickly to her room, changed into trousers and walking shoes and hurried down to meet Harry.

It was so good to be outside in the fresh air. She liked Harry Crawford. He was younger than Ethan, nearer her own age and, on the few times they had met, she'd discovered he was good company.

At the top of the cliff, Kate slung her bag

securely over her shoulder and across her chest to leave her hands free for the steep descent. It had rained overnight and the path could be slippery. She would need to be careful. The day had turned chilly and there was a cold north-east wind blowing in from the sea. Kate shivered. How different it was from the day she came down here with Ethan. Was it really only a few days ago they had walked across the beach together?

When she reached the chapel Harry was standing by his car talking into his mobile.

'Sorry to keep you waiting,' she said, when he had finished. 'I had a bit of trouble finding the file.'

'That's okay. I'm grateful to you for fetching it for me.'

She handed it over.

He opened it up and gave the contents a quick glance, then passed an envelope of odd papers back to her.

'You'd better have this back,' he said. 'It's nothing to do with the chapel.'

She gave it a quick glance. 'Oh, thanks. I must have picked it up by mistake.'

'Shall we get started? Oh - by the way, Ethan asked me to tell you he'll be back this evening. He tried to call you but the phone was engaged and he had to get to a meeting.

Ethan was coming home. In a few hours he would be here. Kate found her mind wandering and was glad Harry was not asking her to do anything that required too much concentration.

Kate followed Harry, taking down notes and measurements as he worked his way round the building. The spiders had been busy over the years and the results of their spinning were everywhere, strung across the windows and walls, leaving great hammocks of dust-laden cobweb hanging from corners and beams. But the building was in surprisingly good condition.

They reached the small alcove leading to the vestry. There were signs of old hinges on one side of the arched entry, suggesting that it had indeed once had a door. An ideal place for storing contraband goods. More recently it had clearly been used as a store for odd items of furniture. Some wooden chairs, an old sofa, some bookshelves, and various other bits and pieces were stacked against one wall.

This must be where Caroline had entertained her lover. Probably on the old sofa. It was certainly long enough for the purpose. She felt a shaft of anger strike through her at the thought. How would she, herself, have felt, had she come in here and found her husband with another woman? Not actually having a husband, she couldn't possibly know. But she could imagine. And in that instant, she felt she understood, as closely as she would ever be able to understand, how Ethan must have felt.

'Kate, did you get that?'

Harry's voice cut into her thoughts. She shook herself and lifted her pencil.

'Sorry, Harry. What did you say?'

'What were you dreaming about? You were miles away.'

'Oh, nothing.' She shrugged it off, wondering if Harry realised the significance of this part of the chapel. But of course he wouldn't. Ethan hadn't told anyone about it. Apart from Ethan and herself, only Vanessa knew. 'Do you believe the past can leave its impression on buildings, Harry? I mean the atmosphere of a place. I can almost feel the presence of the smugglers.'

Harry grinned and raised his arms, making claws of his fingers, as if about to pounce on her. 'Ah-ha,' he joked, putting on a phoney local accent. 'It be the magic o' the Moor. They do say it do get to 'ee arter a while.'

Kate laughed. 'Oh, they do, do they? I think maybe it's got to you.' She paused. Then, 'Harry,' she said quietly, 'what was Ethan's wife like?'

CHAPTER 10

As soon as the words were out, she regretted them. What would Harry think of her asking about the boss's wife? But Harry didn't seem to see anything odd in her question.

He shook his head. 'I don't really know. I never met her.'

'But you've worked for Ethan for some years, haven't you? How can you not have met her?'

'There aren't many round here who have. She'd been abroad for some years and only been back a couple of weeks before she moved to London. She didn't like country life and, from what I hear,' Harry gave a wry grin, 'she wasn't the sort to mix with the yokels. I doubt anyone round here saw much of her apart from Vanessa. And Ruby, I suppose.'

'But she lived here after the wedding?'

'The wedding was in London and they spent most of their time in the London flat. I think they came back here for a few days but all I know is that soon after that she disappeared and Ethan sued for divorce. However, it's not something Ethan ever talks about.'

'And we shouldn't be either. I'm sorry. It was wrong of me to ask you.'

Harry smiled. 'Don't worry. I confess to being a mite curious myself.' He looked at his watch. 'It's getting on. Let's get this finished, shall we?'

For the next hour or so, Kate concentrated her attention on work. She regretted having raised the subject of Caroline and hoped that she had not created more problems by speaking of it to Harry. But he seemed to have put it from his mind and they completed the work without mentioning it again.

Harry packed away the equipment in his case. 'Now, how about some lunch? I don't know about you but my stomach feels as though my throat's been cut.'

'Me, too. I could do with …' she broke off as she heard the sound of a car. I wonder who that is. Are you expecting anyone?'

'Not that I can recall.'

Her heart leapt. 'Perhaps it's Ethan.'

'I doubt it. When he rang earlier he was expecting the meeting to go on until lunch time.'

Kate moved to the doorway of the chapel as the sound of the engine drew closer. She heard the scrunch of tyres on the loose surface of the lane. Then she caught her breath as a silver-grey car nosed round the corner.

Her heart hammered against her ribs. This

couldn't be happening. Please don't let this be what I think it is. The car slowed and pulled up in front of her.

Only one person she knew drove a silver BMW. Richard.

Frozen to the spot, she opened her mouth to speak but the words stuck in her throat. She could only watch, stunned, as he climbed out of the car and strolled towards her, holding out his hands, and smiling as if it was the most natural thing in the world for him to turn up, unannounced and uninvited.

'Katie.' He hadn't changed. Still the same smooth, charming Richard. With a massive ego that just couldn't accept that she wanted nothing more to do with him.

'Katie, it's wonderful to see you. You have no idea how much I've missed you.'

He was about to take her hand. He was leaning towards her. Getting closer. My God, surely he wasn't meaning to kiss her? Surely even he couldn't be that insensitive?

'Kate.' She realised Harry was standing next to her. 'Kate, is everything all right?'

She had to stay calm and play it down. The last thing she wanted was for this to get back to Ethan. If she could just get Richard to leave …

Fighting to control her voice, she said, 'It's okay, Harry. Thanks. This is, er, an ex-colleague of mine. We worked together in London.'

Harry didn't look convinced and gave them

both a searching look. 'Well, if you're sure. I need to get back to the office so if you want a lift ...'

'I'll run her back,' Richard cut in.

'There's no need. I'll walk.' She was tempted to go with Harry but, first, she had to make sure that Richard left and that he wouldn't come back.

Harry was watching her uncertainly.

'It's okay, Harry. Really. You go. I'll be fine. I have my mobile with me if I need to contact you.'

She waited until Harry had driven off down the lane, then, 'What the hell do you think you're doing here?' The words spat out with all the pent up fury she had been suppressing for days. She hadn't realised until this minute just how much his continual pestering had been stressing her.

To her amazement, he actually managed to look hurt. As though he was the injured party, not her. 'But didn't you get my message?' he said. 'Didn't the housekeeper tell you I rang?'

She couldn't believe it. The gall of the man!

'Didn't you get *my* message? *All* my messages?'

'Of course. That's why I've come to see you.'

'But I told you we were finished. That I wanted nothing more to do with you. Surely I made it plain enough?'

'I thought if we could talk, you know, spend some time together, we could work things out.'

'Look,' Kate took a deep breath and said, slowly and deliberately, 'I do not want to talk. There's nothing to talk about. And I certainly do not want to spend any more time with you. You had your chance in London and you blew it. Now, please, just go away.'

'But I love you, Katie. I really do.

'Huh! Well you certainly didn't behave as though you did.'

'I just didn't realise then how much I loved you. But I do now.'

'I see.' Kate's voice was cold. 'Now you've tried every girl in the office, you've decided to come back to me, have you?'

'I know I behaved badly and you have every right to be angry. All I ask is another chance.'

She hardly believe her ears. Was he really so thick-skinned? 'Richard,' she spoke the words emphatically. 'Listen to me. I don't love you. I never did. I realise that now. What I felt for you was no more than infatuation.'

'How can you be so sure?'

'How?' Exasperated, she flung the words at him. 'Because I'm in love with someone else.'

If the situation hadn't been so serious, she might have laughed. Richard seemed to deflate in front of her eyes. His face dropped and his expression changed to one of utter disbelief.

'Oh.' The one word was barely a murmur, as though the air had been punched out of him. 'I see.' His face drained of colour and he looked quite unlike his usual bullish, confident self.

At last, the message seemed to have got through.

Kate began to feel more in control of the

situation. Actually began to feel a little sorry for him. She'd had no idea his feelings had been so strong. It had never occurred to her he might truly love her. Perhaps they could, after all, resolve this situation and part as friends.

Impulsively, she reached out and put a hand on his arm and just as she did so, the first few drops of rain began to fall.

She looked up at the gathering clouds. This wasn't going to be any quick shower. It had all the signs of being a downpour and she didn't have a waterproof with her.

Richard shivered. 'We're going to get soaked out here,' he said. 'Let's get in the car.'

There was no way she was going to do that. 'I can shelter inside the chapel.'

'I can't just leave you here,' Richard said as they dashed inside. 'You'll get soaked if you walk back in this.'

'I'll wait until it stops. Or I can phone Harry and he'll come and fetch me.'

It was chilly inside now the sun had gone in and Kate shivered. Then a thought occurred to her. 'How did you know where I was?' she asked.

'Laura told me.'

'Ah. I might have known.' Her fellow junior editor had never been able to keep anything to herself. And she'd always had a huge crush on Richard, so it wouldn't have taken much effort on his part to persuade her to talk. 'But how did you find me down here? It's not exactly on the main road.'

'You can say that again. It's a miracle the car is still in one piece. I called at the house and some woman gave me directions.'

Kate felt a tremor of unease. Vanessa or Ruby? Not that it made any difference. So much for keeping Richard's visit from Ethan. Either way he was bound to find out now.

'So who is he, then?' Richard's words broke into her thoughts.

'Who's who?'

'Who's the lucky man? My rival?'

'Rival? You don't have a rival.' The man was exasperating. 'If you must know, it's my employer's nephew.'

'Heavens, that was quick. You've only been here a matter of weeks.'

'Sometimes it happens like that.'

His look was searching and she felt herself warming under his gaze. Richard was right. It was very quick and, in view of what had happened between her and Ethan this morning, she felt a moment's uncertainty. Was it, perhaps, too quick? Too soon to really know a man well enough to commit to spending the rest of your life with him? She dismissed the doubts. She loved Ethan with all her heart.

'Katie, don't take this the wrong way but …'

She interrupted him. 'I know what you're going to say and, yes, I am quite sure.'

'There's no hope for me, then.'

'That's what I've been trying to tell you. I'm sorry.'

He gave her a crooked grin. 'I've made a bit of a fool of myself, haven't I?'

Kate smiled and nodded. 'I suppose I should feel flattered that you've been so persistent.'

'I really do love you, you know. I realised as soon as you left London. I could have kicked myself for letting you get away.'

'Even if I had stayed, it wouldn't have worked.' She spoke gently. 'What I felt for you wasn't love and never would have been. I was fond of you and we could have been good friends. But that was all. I know, now, what real love is. And so will you, one day.'

'All I can say is, he's a lucky guy. He must be pretty special.'

Kate nodded. 'Yes. He is.'

'So you'll be staying down here in the back of beyond?'

'I hope so. I love it here.'

'Well, I hope you'll be truly happy.' He shrugged. 'I guess I'd better be on my way. I'm beginning to feel slightly surplus to requirements.'

They faced each other for a moment, then Richard gave her a sheepish grin. 'Can you forgive me for being such an idiot?'

'Of course. I'm just glad that it's sorted at last.'

'I'm really sorry if I caused you problems.'

He could so easily have wrecked things for her with Ethan and she almost told him so, but there was no point in rubbing his nose in it. Soon he would be gone and that would be an end to it. But thank goodness Ethan hadn't been here or things could really have turned nasty.

§

Ethan stopped the Land Rover in front of the house and switched off the windscreen wipers before turning off the engine. For the past hour, he had been driving through torrential rain and some of the side roads were running with streams of thick red water which flooded out onto the main road, making driving hazardous and tiring.

Business in London had gone well and he felt he could leave matters safely in the hands of his managers. He had planned to stay for the week but he was missing Exmoor and Hanging Cross. And, most of all, he found he was missing Kate. She had been on his mind all the time he was away and, for the first time in his life, he'd had difficulty concentrating on business.

The meeting this morning had finished earlier than expected and he'd been able to leave London in good time. The roads had been clear and he'd had a good run home. He was looking forward to surprising Kate.

Two large boxes on the back seat of the Land Rover were full of the work he'd decided to bring home with him. He really must do something about finding a temp. It wasn't fair to expect Kate to keep working extra hours. He would get on to it first thing this afternoon while Kate was with Vanessa.

However, right now, he needed to stretch his legs after the drive. He'd been thinking a lot about the plans for the chapel and had several ideas knocking around in his head. He was excited about the project. It was a new beginning and the future was becoming something to look forward to.

He jumped out, collected his bags and strode into the kitchen.

'Ruby,' he called.

There was no answer. Where was everyone?

He left his things on the chair and went to the office.

It was empty.

Strange. There didn't seem to be anyone around. He guessed Vanessa was out with the dogs. She often took a walk after lunch and that would account for their absence. But it was odd that Kate wasn't here.

He shrugged. He would drive down to the chapel. He wanted to check out some of the ideas he had, but it would have been good to have Kate with him to share the ideas with.

He took his old wax jacket from the back of the door and shrugged into it. The rain had stopped but it was still cold and it would be even colder down there.

He hoped that Harry had made progress on repairing the old road so that they had vehicle access for the main renovation work. He should have done it long ago, before it deteriorated so far. Now he felt an enthusiasm he had never felt before and he knew it was thanks to Kate.

He was looking forward to seeing her again and was surprised how disappointed he felt to find that she wasn't there when he arrived.

The last few yards of road to the chapel were still un-surfaced so he pulled over to the side of the road and stopped. The rain was easing. He would walk the rest of the way.

The men must have gone to lunch. There was no sign of anyone except for a car he didn't recognise parked in front of the chapel.

Whoever it belonged to must be inside.

The door was closed but he could hear voices. He turned the handle and pushed the door open.

§

Kate was relieved that Richard at last seemed to understand the situation and she need no longer worry about him. Impulsively, she reached out and dropped a quick kiss on his cheek and, as Richard bent to return the kiss …

She spun round, heart racing, as a draught of cold air scythed through the room from the open door.

'Ethan.' The word was a cry of dismay.

Why was he here? He wasn't due back until this evening.

§

Ethan felt a white-hot sheet of anger sear through him.

No! It couldn't be happening again. But it was. He felt his muscles tighten as he clenched his fists. Shock, like a pain, scorched along his nerves to his brain.

And in that same second Kate looked up and their eyes met. He noted the horror in hers. No doubt, the horror of being discovered.

He had to get out. Get away. He turned and blindly retraced his steps to where he had left his car, fighting to control the fury and the bitter sense of betrayal that threatened to explode within him.

Adrenalin pumping, a mist of fury blurring his sight, he slammed his foot down on the accelerator and sent the Land Rover screaming back up the lane. Just before the junction with the coast road, he stopped, manoeuvred the car so it was blocking the road, and waited.

§

Frantically, Kate pushed Richard away. The envelope fell from her hands and the contents scattered, flapping across the floor in the breeze from the open door. She watched in a daze as Richard quickly gathered them up and thrust them into her hands.

She saw him register the look of horror on her face. 'Whatever's the matter?'

'That was Ethan. He saw us.'

'But surely if you explain …'

She cut him off. 'Oh, you don't understand. You have no idea. It won't matter what I say. He'll never believe me.'

'Why ever not?'

'Because, thanks to your persistent phone calls, he already thinks we are still in some sort of relationship.' She knew she was shouting but she didn't care. 'I managed to convince him that you meant nothing to me but how do you think this is going to seem to him? He comes home unexpectedly, to find us kissing. Do you think he'll believe it wasn't planned?'

She was beginning to feel hysterical. She just wished that Richard would go. That he had never come in the first place. How was she going to convince Ethan this was an innocent meeting? It would be impossible.

What could she do? There was no point in running after him. He could be miles away by now.

'I'm sorry,' Richard was saying. 'I shouldn't have come. This is my fault.'

Then he was sprinting to his car and the next moment he had gone.

Kate stood alone in the empty yard, feeling wretched and heart-sick. She had no doubt how it must have appeared to Ethan. He would have seen her apparently in the arms of another man and exchanging kisses.

Would he have guessed it was Richard? Oh, yes. He would immediately have put two and two together and made five.

Now he would not only think she was still continuing a relationship with Richard but also that she had lied to him when she told him it was over. So, in Ethan's eyes, she would be both unfaithful and a liar.

§

Ethan did not want to believe what he had just seen. He refused to believe it.

Kate had been telling him the truth when she said she hadn't encouraged Richard. He'd seen the evidence with his own eyes. It was all there in those messages. But clearly this man wasn't going to take no for an answer and if Kate couldn't deal with him then he would have to do it for her.

This time he wasn't going to just walk away.

This time he was going to face it head on.

Sooner or later, Richard would have to drive up this lane and when he did, he would be ready for him.

He opened the door of the Land Rover and stepped out. Closing the door behind him, he leant against the side of his car, eyes fixed on the road, and waited.

The wait was short. No more than ten minutes.

The BMW rounded the last bend, slowed, and came to a halt, it's bonnet only inches away from Ethan.

For a moment neither man moved, then

Richard climbed out to meet him.

Ethan could feel his fists clenching, his fingers flexing and stretching, the pressure in his chest building until he knew something was going to have to give.

He waited, motionless, not speaking, as Richard walked towards him, came closer, hands spread in a gesture of - what? Regret? Apology? Submission? It made no difference. The man had gone too far.

As soon as he was near enough, Ethan let fly. Years of pent-up anger fuelled the blow and an enormous feeling of release flowed through him as his fist made contact and Richard staggered backwards and slowly sank to the ground.

Rubbing his bruised knuckles, Ethan stood and watched, saying nothing, waiting for his anger to abate. Waiting to see how the other man would react.

Richard shook his head and slowly heaved himself up. A little unsteadily, he stood, bracing himself against the side of the BMW. Gingerly, he wiped the back of his hand across his face and, seeing the blood, took out a handkerchief and held it to his nose. 'Okay,' he said, 'I guess I deserved that. I know how it must seem but, believe me, you have nothing to worry about.'

Ethan was surprised at Richard's conciliatory tone but was it just a ploy to allay his suspicions? 'Oh, really,' he growled. 'You expect me to believe that?'

§

Stunned, Kate watched as Richard's car vanished from sight.

A part of her regretted not following her first instinct to run after Ethan. Maybe she could have caught his attention and persuaded him to stop and see reason. Heaven only knew where he was now, or what he would be doing and thinking.

Her legs were shaking; her whole body beginning to tremble. She supposed it must be shock. In less than an hour, her whole life seemed to have crumbled into disaster. Ethan's early home-coming following so close after Richard's unexpected arrival was just too much. She sank down onto one of the pews.

She had almost forgotten the envelope she was holding until she felt it slipping from her fingers. She grabbed at it but missed, and it slid from her lap spilling its contents back onto the floor.

With a sigh, she pushed herself off the pew and knelt down to gather them up. They were of little interest and, as she shook the dust off them one at a time, she barely gave them a second glance ...

Until she saw the photograph.

Dazed, she looked at it for several seconds, her already numbed mind struggling to absorb the implications of what she was seeing. Hastily she shoved the rest of the papers back in the envelope and sat down again, her head spinning.

It wasn't a particularly good photograph,

slightly out of focus and apparently taken in bad light, but there was no doubt about its subject matter. And it must have been taken covertly because she certainly had never been aware of it.

She stared at it, racking her brain for a possible explanation.

Parts of it were blurred but the face that stared back at her from the print was unmistakeably her own; her hair, her eyes looking into the camera.

A chill shivered down her spine as she looked at it.

Why would Ethan have a photograph of her in his desk? And how, and when, had it been taken? If he had wanted a photo of her, he could have taken it openly. There was no need for him to have been secretive about it.

Idly, she turned it in her fingers as the questions raced through her head.

There was a date on the back.

But this was impossible. It must be wrong.

The photograph had been taken more than a year ago. Long before she had come to Hanging Cross.

There was something very strange going on here and she needed answers. Right now. She shoved everything into her bag and slung it across her shoulder.

She had to get back to the house. Somehow she felt sure that Vanessa would have the answers. Odd memories, snippets of conversations, flashed through Kate's mind. Ruby's reaction when she had first arrived. Vanessa's reaction when they had met at the interview. She had thrust them all aside believing she was imagining things. But this photograph told its own story and Kate was determined to get to the bottom of it.

She pulled out her mobile to phone Harry, then put it away again. There was no need to bother him. She could take the cliff path.

The tide was out but the shingle was still wet from the rain. Several times, she almost turned her ankle as she hurried across the loose stones. As she started up the path, a few drops of rain began to fall again. She looked up at the darkening sky. If she didn't hurry, she was going to get a soaking.

What a fool she was not have brought a waterproof with her.

She pressed on, careless of the worsening state of the path. Her only aim was to get back to the house and find Vanessa. Rain sluiced over the stepping stones turning them glossy silvery-grey, and rivulets of red mud trickled between the rocks.

She was breathing hard by the time she reached the top. The muscles of her legs screamed with the strain of keeping her balance but she had made it. Only a few feet to go and she was on level ground.

But relief made her careless.

Wind blew her hair across her eyes. Temporarily blinded, she shook her head to clear her vision.

The movement tipped her balance and she felt

her feet slip from under her.

She was precariously near the edge of the cliff. She threw out her arms in an attempt to break her fall. But there was nothing she could do.

Pain knifed through her as her head made contact with rock.

CHAPTER 11

Slowly, Kate sat up. She felt slightly dizzy but nothing seemed to be broken. Carefully, she eased herself to safety away from the cliff edge. She shuddered to think how easily she might have ended up on the beach far below.

Her head throbbed where she had hit it. Gingerly, she felt the area. There was a lump under her hair but her fingers came away dry so at least it wasn't bleeding. No harm done. She had been lucky.

She got to her feet. Her legs wobbled and, for a second, she felt her head spin alarmingly. She stood quietly until the ground stopped moving. It wasn't too far to go and if she took it steadily, she would be fine.

By the time she reached the house, she had regained her equilibrium and, apart from the pounding in her head and a few aches, she felt fine. It must have been shock that had made her feel shaky.

There was no sign of Ethan's car in the yard and she wondered if he had come back to the house. No doubt she would find out when she saw Vanessa.

The door to the estate office was open and the room was empty. She might as well return the papers. She dropped everything except the photograph onto Ethan's desk. Then she took a mirror from her bag and checked her face. The lump on her head was concealed by her hair but a smear of mud clung to her cheek. She wiped it off with a tissue and ran a comb through her hair, grimacing as it pulled at her scalp. She felt better.

Now, to find Vanessa and get those answers.

Nervously, wondering what she might be about to learn, she knocked on Vanessa's door, feeling a sudden surge of anger towards her. Her feelings must have shown on her face as she entered the room because Vanessa looked startled and asked, 'Is something wrong?'

Kate had no intention of beating about the bush.

She held up the photograph. 'I thought perhaps you could explain this.'

Vanessa turned pale as the blood drained from her face and for a moment Kate thought she was going to faint. Her words, when she eventually replied, were spoken so quietly Kate could barely hear what she was saying.

'Oh lord. I suppose you were bound to find out eventually. I had hoped … Oh, I don't know. It all seems so …' She sighed. 'I realise now that it was very silly of me.'

'Vanessa, what on earth has been going on? Why would Ethan have a photograph of me in his desk? One I wasn't even aware he had taken?'

Vanessa looked taken aback. 'A photo of you?'

'Yes. A photo of me.' Kate waved the photograph. 'This photo. I found it in his desk.'

'Oh, but ...' Vanessa seemed at a loss for words. She stood up and wandered across to the window, nervously folding and unfolding her arms. She stood looking out at the garden.'

'Vanessa,' Kate prompted. 'Please tell me.'

At last, Vanessa seemed to come to a decision. 'Come with me,' she said. 'There is something I think you should see.'

Mystified, Kate followed her into the hall and up the stairs and, as they started up the second flight, she realised they were heading for the attics. She had never been up here before and was surprised to find how vast they were. Under the sloping roof, a series of rooms led one through another, each containing stored furniture, boxes, and various household items. Cedarwood cupboards lined some of the walls and one of the doors stood open giving a glimpse of racks of clothes, presumably the ones Vanessa and her brother, Charles, had used for dressing up in. At any other time, Kate would have found it fascinating. Now she could think of nothing but the mystery of the photograph.

Vanessa opened a door and beckoned her through into the room beyond. Kate looked around. An old oak desk and a large chest of drawers stood against one wall next to a dormer window that overlooked the yard in front of the house and the drive down from the moor. Stacked against the remaining walls, and covered with dust and cobwebs, were dozens of paintings, many of them in heavy ornate frames.

'Welcome to the Cade family archives.' Vanessa indicated the room with a sweep of her arm. 'This is where all the family records are kept.'

'But what has this to do with me?' Kate was puzzled.

'Somewhere in here is a portrait which, if I can find it …' Vanessa's voice trailed off as her eyes scanned the room. The paintings had been stacked with their faces to the wall and it took some moments searching through them before Vanessa found what she was looking for. 'Ah, there it is.' She crossed to where some more modern frames were stacked and pulled one out. 'This is what I want to show you.'

Wondering what she was going to see, Kate watched as Vanessa stood the painting on the floor, leaning against the chest, and turned it round to face her.

For a moment Kate thought she was looking in a mirror. Stunned, she gazed at the portrait in front of her. There it was again. The same hair, the same eyes, the shape of the face, everything just the same.

It was her.

Yet it wasn't her.

She looked closer. At the foot of the portrait was the artist's signature and under that, the name of the woman.

Suddenly, everything became blindingly clear. This was the reason Ethan had been acting so strangely ever since she had arrived.

The portrait wasn't of her at all.

It was a portrait of Caroline.

Kate looked again at the photograph she had brought with her. It wasn't of herself. She could see that now. The photo, too, was of Caroline.

The bright auburn curls, the green eyes, the shape of her face. They were almost identical to her own. They could have been sisters - twins even. They say everyone has a double somewhere and this was certainly hers.

This explained so much.

She turned accusingly to Vanessa.

'This is why you gave me that strange look at the interview, isn't it? I sensed something was odd at the time but then decided I must have imagined it.'

'You're right. I thought I was seeing things when you walked in. For a second, I even thought you were Caroline.'

'Then why did you offer me the job? I don't understand. You must have known it would cause problems?'

'I know. I should have told you straight away that you weren't suitable. Found some reason.

Thought up some excuse. In fact, I almost did. But, you see, you were so right for the job, and I liked you immensely, even at that first meeting. I suppose I was afraid that, if you knew, you would turn me down.'

Kate lifted her hand in protest. 'There must have been more to it than that. I'm sure you had plenty of applicants to choose from. There must be no end of people who would jump at the chance to work here. Please, Vanessa. Tell me the real reason.'

Vanessa shuffled uneasily from one foot to the other, like a child caught in the act of doing something it shouldn't.

'You're right, of course.' She paused and thought, then spoke softly, looking at Kate as if willing her to understand. 'I'm afraid this is going to sound terribly selfish. I love my nephew. He and I are all we've got. I never married, you see. Never had children of my own.'

Her eyes glazed for a moment as if remembering something long gone and Kate had a sense of some deep sadness in Vanessa's past and wondered why this warm-hearted woman had remained single. Maybe this was what gave her novels such depth and feeling.

'Charles never really wanted children,' Vanessa continued. 'All he was interested in was getting an heir. He packed Ethan off to boarding school when he was six and proceeded to drink and gamble his life away. He made no secret of his womanising and his wife tolerated it and stayed with him for the child's sake. So all Ethan ever knew of family life was what he saw in the school holidays. A dissolute father who openly flaunted his mistresses, and a desperately unhappy mother.'

'But I still don't see what all this has got to do with me.'

Vanessa turned and stared out of the dormer window. 'Since they died, it's been just the two of us. I came to live here to run the house so Ethan could put all his energies into building up the estate and the business. He was so driven that I began to fear that he would never settle down. Never be really happy. Oh, he had no shortage of women willing to go out with him but no-one he was ever serious about. He could never forget his parent's miserable life, you see. Then he met Caroline and everything changed. He fell hook, line and sinker, as they say. For a while he was different person. So content. So much in love.' She sighed and turned back to face Kate. 'Well, you know what happened next. After that, he just withdrew into himself. I couldn't bear to see him so dreadfully unhappy.

'Then I met you. And you looked so like her that I thought maybe he would feel about you as he had felt about Caroline. Oh,' she hurried on as Kate opened her mouth to speak. 'I know now it was a stupid idea.'

'You're darned right it was.' Kate could hardly believe she was hearing this. 'It was far more likely to have the opposite effect! Which it did. No wonder he looked shocked when he saw me.'

It was all beginning to fall into place. The strange looks. Ruby's comments when she first saw her. Ethan's reaction when she took off her hat and he saw her hair. No wonder his attitude had changed.

Impulsively, Vanessa moved forward and took Kate's hand. 'Oh, my dear, I'm so very sorry. What a mess I've made of things.'

Kate shrugged her hand free. Mixed emotions of sympathy and anger churned through her. Anger at the knowledge that she had been used.

'How did you think you were going to get away with it?' she asked. 'I mean, why hasn't somebody said anything to me? I can't believe no-one has noticed. What about Ruby?'

Vanessa looked sheepish. 'I'm afraid I swore Ruby to secrecy. She wasn't happy about it but, as you've probably realised, she would do just about anything for Ethan. She took some persuading though.'

'And Ethan? Why hasn't he said anything?'

'Pride, my dear. It would have meant him explaining to you about Caroline and that is something he never talks about.'

A memory stirred in Kate's mind. A vague recollection of something Ethan had said to her, she couldn't quite remember when, about wanting to tell her something but not being able to. Was this what he had been referring to? But there were other people. Villagers, workers.

'What about the estate workers?'

'I'm not sure any of them saw Caroline that closely. She wasn't one to mix with the 'servants' as she called them, and the whole affair was over so quickly that she only lived here for a few days.' She shrugged her shoulders. 'We're pretty isolated here and I suppose I just kept my fingers crossed that, by the time anyone commented, you and Ethan would be - well, you know ...'

Her voice trailed off.

The full implication of her discovery suddenly hit Kate. She felt it like a weight in her chest and, to her fury, her eyes filled and blurred.

'You realise I'll have to go,' she whispered, swallowing the lump that had risen to her throat, fighting to control the threatening tears.

'Go? Go where? What on earth are you talking about?'

'I have to, Vanessa.' With the shock of Vanessa's confession, she had completely forgotten that Vanessa knew nothing of the events of the past few hours. In the light of what she had just learned she realised that any chance of reconciliation with Ethan was impossible.

It was all too much and, to her horror, she realised that tears were pouring down her face. But she was past caring. All she knew was that she had to get away before Ethan returned. There was no way she could face him again after this.

'But Ethan loves you, I'm sure of it. I've seen the way he looks at you. And you love him, too.

Surely we can work something out?'

'No. It's impossible. How can I stay after this? Knowing every time he looks at me he is seeing Caroline? How will he ever forget her with me here as a constant reminder?'

'You couldn't be more different to Caroline, and Ethan knows that.'

'He doesn't. He thinks I'm having an affair with Richard.'

'Why on earth would he think that?'

'Because he saw Richard kissing me.'

Vanessa stared in horror as Kate told her what had happened.

'Oh, my dear, surely he will understand if you explain. It's hardly your fault if this man persists in making a nuisance of himself.'

'I don't think. …'

Kate broke off as she heard the sound of car tyres on the gravel drive. She flew to the window.

'It's Ethan. He's back. I must go.'

Vanessa looked out. 'He's going to the stables. I expect he will ride up to the moor. It's what he usually does when he has something on his mind.'

'Good. That gives me plenty of time to pack and go before he gets back.'

Without waiting to hear Vanessa's reply, Kate turned and strode from the room. The sudden turn made her head swim and she swayed slightly.

'Kate, is something wrong? Are you feeling unwell?'

'I'm fine.' All she could think of was that she

had to leave Hanging Cross and she had to go now, before she had to face Ethan again.

Her emotions were all over the place. Seeing her likeness to Caroline had been an enormous shock and, knowing what Ethan must have being going through every time he looked at her, she could feel compassion for him. At the same time, she was mad at him for not trusting her and telling her about this. Surely he could see that just because she happened to look like Caroline, didn't mean that she was going to act like her?

And how Vanessa could have acted so thoughtlessly, she couldn't understand.

The more she thought about it, the more angry she became. None of this was her fault but she was the one who was being made to pay for it.

Well she wasn't going to hang around where she wasn't wanted. She was off. Right now.

Back in her own room, she pulled her suitcase from the wardrobe and threw it onto the bed. Adrenalin coursed through her making her taught and edgy as though she had drunk too much coffee. She wrenched open drawers and flung their contents roughly into the case. Her only thought was to get away without being seen.

Somehow, she managed to cram everything into her case and a holdall. She didn't want to have to make two journeys to the car.

She took a last look round the room. How different everything had seemed when she first arrived. It had seemed the answer to her dreams.

Instead it had become a nightmare.

With a shrug, she picked up her bags. Time to go.

She opened the bedroom door and paused. All was quiet. In her present mood she really didn't want to meet anyone. Carefully, she made her way down the stairs, saying a silent goodbye to the family as they gazed at her from their ornate frames on stair wall.

By the time she reached the hall, she was beginning to feel light-headed again. But it was only a short way from there to her car and once she was in and sitting down, the dizziness would go and she would be fine.

She slipped silently through the open back door and crossed the yard, hoping Ethan had indeed gone riding. At all costs, she had to avoid meeting him. The gravel crunched beneath her feet but no-one came out to question her.

The ancient Fiesta seemed like an old friend waiting to welcome her. Thankfully, she opened the door, threw her bags inside and slid into the driver's seat. She closed her eyes for a second but it made the dizziness worse and she swallowed hard as a wave of nausea surged through her.

Air. She needed air. She wound down the window and took a deep breath. Better.

She turned the key. The noise of the engine thundered through the silence. She glanced round but no-one seemed to have heard it.

She slammed the gear into first and almost

stalled as her foot jerked on the clutch. Panicking and expecting at any moment to see Ethan striding across the yard, she pressed the accelerator. The car shot forward. Somehow, she managed to steer through the gates and into the lane.

The high hedges felt like a tunnel as she drove through them, closing over her head, oppressive, cutting out the sun and casting floating shadows across the road. Or was it her imagination? Despite the shade, her face was wet with sweat. She raised her arm to wipe it away with her sleeve. Not sweat. She realised tears were pouring down her cheeks. She hadn't been aware that she was crying.

She was almost at the top of the hill. Almost at the crossroads.

It was such a short time ago that she had arrived here, full of optimism and excitement. Now she was leaving, hurt and heart-sore.

The stone was ahead of her; half concealed in the bracken. The site of the hanging cross; the gibbet upon which so many smugglers had ended their lives.

The hedge-shaded lane was behind her and she was out on the open moor. The sun shining in her eyes momentarily blinded her.

Waves of blackness swam across her vision and her stomach lurched. Oh God, she was going to be sick. Her mouth watered. She swallowed, fighting the churning sensation; willing herself not to throw up.

All she wanted to do was lie down and go to sleep. She felt her eyes begin to close and snapped them open again. Stay awake, stay awake, she repeated to herself.

She struggled to keep the car on the road, but the steering wheel was so heavy she could hardly move it.

Her foot slipped from the accelerator but she barely noticed. What did it matter anyway? She wasn't going anywhere. She was too tired; much too tired to drive. Why bother to stay awake? Why not just close her eyes and rest a while?

She didn't see the horse until it was too late.

She had a fleeting impression of flailing hooves as the horse reared in fright, almost unseating its rider. Instinctively, she wrenched at the steering wheel and the car skidded off the road and into the grass. She was only vaguely aware of the impact before blackness overwhelmed her.

CHAPTER 12

Kate opened her eyes. What had happened? Ah, yes - the stone. Through the fog that clouded her brain, she remembered hitting the stone. The cold steering wheel pressed against her face. Slowly, she pushed herself upright and leant back in the seat. 'Ouch.' Her head was spinning again.

Through the window she could see Mack, snorting and tossing his head as Ethan leapt from the saddle. Talk about history repeating itself. Her heart sank as she remembered the last time she had narrowly missed him on this very same stretch of road. The day she'd arrived at Hanging Cross. If he'd been angry then, what was his reaction going to be now? Not that it mattered now she was leaving anyway.

She jumped as Ethan wrenched open the car door. He stood, legs apart, one hand still on the door, glaring at her. His eyes were dark with fury.

'You stupid woman,' he growled. 'What the hell did you think you were doing?'

Well, that told her everything. Clearly any

feelings he might have had for her had been wiped out by the encounter at the chapel. Well she wasn't going to stand for it. If he truly loved her, he would have believed her when she said she had finished with Richard. Okay, she could imagine what it must have looked like when he saw them both together, but he hadn't even given her a chance to explain before rushing off in a rage. Was that the action of a man in love?

Anger welled up inside her. Anger at herself for allowing the situation to arise in the first place. Anger at him for being so… so…

'Doing? What do you think I was doing?' she snapped. 'Getting away from you, that's what.'

She grabbed the door handle and tried to pull the door from his grasp, to close it against him.

He held on.

'Let go,' she yelled. 'Let me go. How dare you try and stop me.'

'Stop you? You stopped yourself by going off the road. And where did you think you were going anyway?'

'Anywhere,' she spat. 'Away from here. Away from you.'

He looked taken-aback; puzzled. 'Why, for heaven's sake?'

'Why? You have to ask that? That says it all, doesn't it. You're so superior, so sure of yourself. Always right; always in control. Well you might be master of Hanging Cross but you're not my master.' She took a deep breath and reached to turn the ignition key. 'I'm going home.'

His face contorted with anger.

'Don't be ridiculous. You're in no fit state to drive anywhere.'

'I'll manage.'

'I don't think so.' He pointed to the front of the car. 'You'll be lucky if you get half a mile with that radiator.'

It was a trick. It must be. There was nothing wrong with the radiator. It was a ploy to stop her leaving. Although why he would want to do that, she couldn't imagine.

'I don't believe you.'

He let go of the door and stepped back from the car, spreading his arms in an expression of resignation. 'Have it your own way.'

Kate slammed the door shut. Then hesitated. Suppose the radiator was damaged? It had been quite a jolt when the car hit the stone. Maybe she'd better check just in case. She had nothing to lose. If it was okay then she would have won her point. If it wasn't, then ... well, she supposed she would have to give in gracefully.

She closed her eyes again for a second, willing her still-spinning head to settle, then opened the door, gingerly swung her legs round and slid off the seat. Still holding on to the car for support, she stood up. A bit wobbly; but okay so far. One foot in front of the other, slowly, and she'd be fine. The last thing she was going to do was to betray any sign of weakness in front of him. She rested her hand on the car bonnet as she moved slowly round to the front then bent to examine the radiator. Big mistake. The ground shifted and she swayed as her head, feather-light, floated up into blackness and she was falling.

She felt Ethan's arms catch her. Felt herself pulled close against him. Damn. She struggled, pushing with her hands against his chest.

'Let me go. I'm fine.'

'Like hell you are.'

'How can you possibly know how I feel?'

Roughly, he took her by the shoulders so that he could look at her. His dark eyes raked her face.

'How do you think? You're pale, your cheeks are flushed, your pupils are dilated, you can hardly stand let alone walk. Shall I go on?'

'It's nothing. I banged my head, that's all.'

She lifted her hand to where the lump under hair had resumed its throbbing. She saw Ethan frown and took her hand away but it was too late. Gently, he parted her hair.

'How did you get this?'

Kate shrugged. 'On the steering wheel, I suppose.'

He shook his head. 'Uh-uh. Wrong place. I'd guess this was done a few hours ago. What's been going on?'

What the hell. What did it matter now? 'If you must know, I slipped on the cliff path on my way back to the house. After you'd driven off and left me.'

'What were you doing going that way? Haven't you been here long enough to know how dangerous it can be when it's been raining?'

'How else was I supposed to get back?'

'You should have phoned someone and waited. You're lucky you didn't kill yourself. As it is, it probably gave you concussion. Which would account for your idiotic behaviour. Whatever possessed you to try and drive?'

Impatiently, she shrugged away from him. He was right, of course. Not that she was going to admit it. He was right about the radiator, too. So what did she do now? Walk? If only she didn't feel so tired. She turned her back on him and braced herself against the bonnet of the car, willing her legs not to give way.

She sensed Ethan move behind her. Felt his breath on her neck as he leant towards her and pulled her closer. His strong arms clasped her tightly as he turned her round to face him. She kept her head down, not daring to look at him. How could she resist this man when she loved him so much? When just by touching her, he sapped her of her will-power.

His hand was under her chin, tilting her face upwards so their eyes met, and what she saw there made her catch her breath. His eyes, those deep, dark, beautiful eyes, held an expression she thought she would never see again. In an instant, the atmosphere between them changed. The sounds and stirrings of the moor, faded into the background. The wind stilled. The birds stopped singing. The crash of waves on the shingle far below faded to a distant murmur. The air between them was electric with expectation. Time was on hold.

Ethan's gaze held hers. She was like a moth caught in a flame, sensing danger but unable to move away. She could hear the thump of her own heart beating in her head. She took a deep breath to try and calm her racing pulse and trembled as the warm male scent of him flooded through her.

Ethan pulled her close. His voice was husky as he spoke. 'You're cold.'

She was afraid to shake her head, afraid to speak in case her voice gave her away, so she said nothing. The intensity of her body's reaction to his touch was overwhelming as she felt the familiar delicious stirrings in the pit of her stomach and the tingling warmth flooding through her whole being.

She made no protest when he gently stroked her bruised forehead. 'Enough of this,' he said, 'I'm taking you home. Do you think you can ride?' He reached for his mobile. 'Or shall I phone for someone to fetch us?'

'No.' She didn't want to share him. Didn't want to break the spell. 'I'll be fine. But what about my car?'

'It's not going anywhere. Forget it. I'll send someone up for it later.' He took hold of her arm and led her to where Mack was waiting, quiet now after his fright. 'Hold onto the saddle. I'll give you a leg-up.'

He lifted her up and she grabbed the pommel as Mack sidestepped. Ethan swung up behind her and she gave a sigh of relief as his arms closed round her, holding her safe. She let her head fall back against his shoulder.

'Okay?' he asked.

She could feel the soft movement of his breathing, the strength of his muscles as he clasped her to him. 'Oh, yes,' she whispered.

Ethan urged Mack into a gentle walk and Kate settled back against him, revelling in the sensation of their bodies moving in unison as the horse picked his way down the lane. No other man had ever had the effect on her that Ethan did. Whatever happened between them, however things turned out, she knew she would always love him. Anyone else could only ever be second-best.

She kept silent, wanting to enjoy the moment and acutely aware that this may be the last thing she had to remember him by. Because nothing had really changed. She still had to leave Hanging Cross. But at least they might now part as friends.

Home, he had said. He was taking her home. She wondered what that meant. Was he intending to drive her back to Oxfordshire? She would miss him desperately and miss Hanging Cross but she would remember this ride for ever. Whatever happened now, she would not spoil this moment. She would savour the magic of it for ever.

Even at a walk, Mack covered the distance quickly, too quickly, and it seemed only moments until Ethan halted the horse at the back door of the house and dismounted. As he reached up to help her down, Vanessa came hurrying out to meet them.

Kate stepped down onto the cobbles and Ethan put his hand under her elbow to steady her. Surely this concern was proof that he loved her? It was so tempting to believe what she had read in his eyes. But, no, he would have done as much for anyone who needed help. And she must remember that, even if he did love her, there could be no future for them. The image of Caroline would always be there between them.

The sooner she could make a dignified departure, the better.

Vanessa came round and took her other arm, worry creasing her kindly face. 'Whatever has happened?'

To Kate's relief, Ethan replied for her. 'It's all right, Nessa. A bit of an accident with the car. There's nothing to worry about. Can you take Kate inside? I must see to Mack but I won't be long.'

Kate followed Vanessa through the kitchen and into the sitting room. It was a relief to sink into the soft, saggy sofa and curl up in front of the fire. She shivered and Vanessa pulled a warm throw from one of the chairs and tucked it round her.

'I'll be back in a moment,' she told her. 'I'm

going to fetch you a hot drink.'

She disappeared to the kitchen and came back carrying a tray with two mugs of hot chocolate. She put the tray down on a side table. 'This is all my fault, isn't it?' she said as she handed one of the mugs to Kate. 'I don't know how I could have been so foolish.'

Kate sipped her drink. It was warm and soothing. Just what she needed. Vanessa was so clearly distressed, there was no point in upsetting her any further. 'You did what you thought was right,' she told her.

'But the car accident? You could have killed yourself. Thank goodness Ethan found you and brought you back.' She broke off as the door opened and Ethan walked in.

'Ethan,' she said. 'There you are. Are you going to …?'

'Nessa,' Ethan broke in. 'Would you mind giving us a few minutes alone? Please?'

Despite everything, Kate could barely restrain a smile at the look of delighted expectation that crossed Vanessa's face as she glanced from Ethan to her. She was incorrigible. Such a pity she was going to be disappointed.

Vanessa patted Ethan's arm and smiled at Kate. 'Of course. I have some work to do, anyway. My heroine seems to have got herself into another sticky situation and I'm not altogether sure how to get her out of it. So I'll see you both later.'

With Vanessa's departure, an awkwardness

settled on the room. There was so much to be said yet neither of them seemed to be able to find the words.

Ethan threw another couple of logs on the fire, sending flames dancing up the chimney.

Eventually, Kate broke the silence. 'There's a hot chocolate there for you.' She nodded towards the tray Vanessa had left on the table. 'Though I'm not sure it will be very hot by now.'

Ethan picked up the mug and frowned and put it down again. 'I think I need something a little stronger,' he said. 'How about you? On second thoughts,' he added, 'alcohol is almost certainly not a good idea for someone with concussion.'

He crossed to the drinks cabinet, poured himself a large whisky and took a gulp.

Kate hugged her knees and stared into the fire. Riding down from the moor, her body against Ethan's as they moved together to the rhythm of Mack's gait, she had felt so at ease with him. But now the room was filled with tension. Had she completely misread the situation?

She finished her drink and leant across to put the empty mug on the table. As she did so, Ethan reached out to take it from her. For an instant they both held it as though hoping it might offer a means of communication. Then Ethan let go and the moment was gone.

He tossed back the rest of his whisky and turned back towards the fireplace, leaning across it, his hands braced against the mantelpiece, his head bowed.

Kate searched for something to say that would ease the tension. But where to begin? If only Ethan would turn and look at her, but he still had his back towards her. The only sounds were the crackle of the logs on the fire and the clock in the corner as it ticked the seconds away. The pressure within her grew until she could stand it no longer. If she didn't do something, she would burst.

Impatiently, she threw the rug from her lap and swung her feet to the floor.

That got his attention. At last he turned and faced her.

They stood, inches apart, the air between them alive with suppressed emotion.

Kate held her breath. The desire to throw her arms round him and bury her face in his chest was almost as irresistible as the urge to throw something at him; to jog him out of this silence; to make him say something. Anything. But there was no way she was going to let her defences down in front of him again. Nothing had changed. Whatever his reaction, whatever he might say to her, she was still going to have to leave Hanging Cross and the only way she was going survive this with her sanity intact was to keep a firm hold on her emotions.

She took a deep breath. She couldn't stay in the same room with him feeling as she did. She would go to her own room and rest and then make a dignified departure in the morning … except that she couldn't, of course. There was the small matter of her car, still up on the moor, wrapped round a rock waiting for someone to fetch it. She mentally shrugged. She would face that problem in the morning.

I'm going upstairs,' she said, turning on her heel.

But the move was too sudden and she swayed. As she fought to keep her balance, Ethan reached out to catch her and before she knew it she was in his arms again, held tight against him, her face cushioned against the rough weave of his sweater, feeling the rise and fall of his chest as he breathed. The temptation to stay there was overwhelming. But she mustn't. If she did, she would be lost. She wriggled her arms free and put her hands against his chest to push him away, but Ethan kept hold of her, his hands firmly on her shoulders.

'You could have killed yourself, going off like that.' His voice was almost a growl. 'What on earth were you thinking of?'

'Thinking of?' Didn't he listen? 'I thought I'd made that plain. I was leaving.'

She tried again to pull away but he held on to her.

'But why? I mean, why then? Like that?'

This time she managed to jerk herself free. Did he really not understand? Surely it must have been obvious, even to him, that it was impossible for her to stay.

In frustration she balled her fists, bringing

them down with force against his chest.

'Because I couldn't bear to be in the same house as you, that's why. I love you and I thought you loved me; but you don't. You didn't trust me, did you? You believed your eyes. Without stopping to think. You saw me with a man and jumped to the first conclusion that hit you, that I was having some sort of relationship with him despite the fact that I had already told you I wanted nothing to do with him. You really thought that I would do something that awful. Well, how do you expect me to live in this house with you knowing you feel like that?'

So much for controlling her emotions. She knew she was shouting but she was beyond caring. She might as tell him straight and be done with it. 'You made it clear enough what you thought of me. You just drove off without waiting to hear what had really happened.'

He grabbed her wrists and moved back, keeping her at arms length. 'I know that's what it must have looked like but ...'

'Looked like?' she interrupted. 'It couldn't have been much plainer.'

'Things aren't always as they seem, as you know only too well. Remember what I thought about Richard's phone calls?'

He was right. He had listened to her explanations about that. He had believed her and apologised.

He released her wrists. 'Now,' he continued,

'perhaps you will do me the courtesy of listening to what I have to say?' He took her hand and pulled her towards the sofa. 'Come and sit down.'

She hesitated.

'Please?' he said.

It wouldn't hurt to listen to what he had to say. She supposed she owed him that much. But she had no intention of relaxing too much. She didn't trust herself or her reactions. Her mind might decide to play it cool but her body had other ideas.

She perched uncomfortably on the edge of the sofa and turned towards him, waiting.

He still had hold of her hand and gently, almost absent-mindedly, he stroked it with his finger. His face creased with concentration as though searching for the right words.

Eventually, he raised his head and looked directly at her.

'I know I over-reacted,' he said. 'You know well enough what happened with Caroline. What happened at the chapel.'

Kate opened her mouth to speak but he stopped her.

'No, please let me finish first. I'd been thinking so much about you, about us, while I was away. In fact I thought about little else.' He gave a brief, wry smile. 'I think it must be the first time in my life I've found it difficult to concentrate on business.

'Anyway, I'd done a lot of thinking about everything we'd discussed and I had some new ideas for the chapel conversion. When I got back from London, I went to look for you, hoping we could go down together and talk them through. But you weren't around so I decided to go down on my own.

'When I saw you inside with Richard, it was as if I'd somehow stepped back in time. It was Caroline and her lover all over again. All I could see was the two of you, standing so close, and I couldn't think straight. I just let my emotions take over.'

'I knew straight away how it must have appeared to you,' Kate said. 'I understood, truly I did. But it wasn't what you thought.'

'I know that. I realised almost immediately that this must be Richard's doing. I also knew that if I stayed a moment longer I would have done something I might have regretted later.'

'So you drove away?'

He nodded. 'And waited for him in the lane.'

Kate caught her breath as her imagination went into overdrive. 'What happened?'

'Don't worry. He's fine - apart from a bloody nose and a bruised ego. Actually, after our initial, er, encounter, we talked. Or rather, he did. He admitted to pestering you. Said you had told him to get lost more than once.'

'He admitted that?'

'He did. He wouldn't have a word spoken against you and insisted it was all a misunderstanding on his part.'

'Well that's one way of putting it, I suppose.

And then what happened?'

'We shook hands and got into our respective cars and he drove off.'

'And why didn't you come back for me?'

'I did, but there was no sign of you so I phoned the house and Vanessa said you were there, so I assumed you had gone with someone else.'

'And how could I have done that without passing you in the lane?'

'I know. I guess I wasn't thinking straight. I was still pretty angry, even after Richard had gone. I'd no idea you might be climbing the cliff path.'

He stroked her hair, where the bruise was staining her skin in shades of purple and green. 'When I think how near I came to losing you. It could have been so much worse than just concussion. I can't bear to think what might have happened if you had slipped right down the cliff.' He made a sound somewhere between a sob and a groan. 'Oh, God. How can I have been so stupid?'

He reached out and pulled her towards him, holding her close, rocking her gently and, against her better judgement, she relaxed into his embrace. She felt his head rest against hers; felt his shuddering breaths as he struggled to control his emotions.

'Can you ever forgive me?' he whispered.

She tried to speak but there seemed to be a lump in her throat. The words refused to come, so she just hugged him and nodded. For precious seconds they revelled in each other's nearness.

Then Kate levered herself free, placing her palm against his chest to hold him at arms length.

'When you didn't come straight back to the house, I thought you were staying away because you were angry with me.'

'I needed to let off steam so I drove up to the moor and walked for a while.' He shrugged. 'It didn't help. All I could think of was the time we went riding up there together. I needed to get my thoughts in order before I came back and saw you.'

'Is that why you drove straight to the stables instead of coming into the house?'

His eyes registered surprise. 'How did you know I did?'

'I saw you. I was up in the attic with Vanessa. The window overlooks the yard.'

Was it her imagination, or did he suddenly look guilty? No - not guilty. Sheepish. Like a small boy caught out in some act of mischief.

'Ah.' It was said so quietly that Kate hardly heard it. 'So you know?'

'I made Vanessa tell me. I found a photograph of Caroline in your desk. At first, I thought it was of me.'

He grimaced. 'I was sure I'd got rid of them all. The last thing I wanted was photos of her all over the place.'

'I guess this one slipped through the net. I'm glad it did. If I hadn't seen it, I would never have believed that two people could look so alike.'

'When we first met, I thought I was seeing

things. When you took off that ridiculous hat you were wearing, it was as though I'd been hit in the stomach; as though Caroline had come back to haunt me.'

She reached for his hand and felt his fingers curl round hers.

'It wasn't just the looks,' he continued, 'the chemistry was there as well.' He looked at her. 'I think you felt it, too?'

She couldn't deny it. The memory of that first encounter was still able to fire the blood in her veins. She nodded. 'Yes, I did.'

'But I thought, then, it was just because you were so like Caroline. I was afraid you might be like her in other respects, too; that if I allowed you to get too close, I would end up … well, you know; once bitten and all that. And I really did not want to be reminded of her all the time. It was a part of my life I had tried to put behind me. So I determined to keep you at arms length.'

'You made a pretty good job of it.'

'It wasn't easy. If you only knew how many times I wanted to take you in my arms and kiss you.'

'If you only knew how many times I wanted you to,' Kate said softly.

'Well, somehow I eventually managed to convince myself you were different. That just because one woman behaves in a certain way, it doesn't mean others will be the same; even if they do look almost identical. Then, after we talked that night, I knew I loved you and I believed you loved me. I was so sure everything would be all right between us.

'And thanks to you I was able to finally lay Caroline's ghost. I suppose that was another reason I went to the chapel when I got back from London. To make sure I hadn't imagined it all. That I had truly succeeded in putting it all behind me. That going there no longer had the power to hurt.'

'And there I was, in another man's arms. Or so you thought.'

'Exactly. Caroline all over again.'

'Ethan.' Kate spoke hesitantly. This was the last thing she wanted to say, yet it had to be said. If she didn't, she would never be sure. He was looking at her, waiting for her to speak, sensing perhaps that she was walking a tightrope. 'Ethan, I do love you. And I believe you love me. But every time you look at me, you see Caroline. She will always be there between us and it will get more difficult as time goes on. I can't stay here, knowing that.'

He looked shocked. 'Was that why you drove off? Because you found out that you looked like Caroline?'

'Surely you can't deny that I remind you of her?'

'No, of course I don't. But you are so different in every other way. You are warm and generous and loyal. I've known you for such a short time, yet I know, without a doubt, that you are everything she was not.' He took her hands, and his eyes scanned her face as if searching for reassurance that she believed him. 'Trust me, my love. You are everything to me.' He touched her lips in a brief kiss. 'I love you.' He kissed her again. 'You cannot leave me now.' His eyes sparked with mischief. 'I am the master here and I forbid it.'

Kate shivered with delight. He was joking - wasn't he?

Her eyes widened. 'The master, eh?' she teased. 'Then I must do as I am told.'

His eyes locked on hers, boring into her very soul, drawing her closer until she stood against him, her body touching his. She lifted her arms and placed her hands behind his head, pulling it down so she could reach his mouth with hers. She felt his arms round her, pulling her even tighter against him.

Their lips touched and his tongue began to explore hers, first gently, then with ever more urgency. He stroked his hands along her back then moved slowly, sensuously up her spine to her neck. His fingers sent shivers of delight through her as they played on the sensitive area around her hairline, and all the time his lips were exploring her mouth, her ears, her eyes. She could feel his arousal, hear the beating of his heart. She was light-headed with desire.

Between kisses he murmured her name.

'My, love,' he whispered. 'Can you forgive me? Can we put all this behind us and begin again?'

She looked into his eyes and saw the barely-controlled passion and love that smouldered there. She now had no doubt that he loved her as much as she loved him. Perhaps they could put the spectre of the past behind them. If they both wanted it badly enough. And she believed that they did.

She ran her fingers over Ethan's face, his eyes, his lips, drinking in every last seductive masculine inch of him.

She smiled as she said, 'Oh, yes.'

He shuddered, and his voice was husky. 'If you don't control your hands, I will not be held responsible for my actions.'

'Mmm,' she teased, 'perhaps I should carry on, then?'

He shuddered. 'In which case, I'm afraid there is only one solution.'

'And what might that be?'

'You will just have to marry me.'

Kate looked at him wide-eyed, pretending to be shocked. 'Isn't there a slight impediment to that course of action?'

'Only for another two weeks. Then I shall be free.'

'Well, it's not much of a proposal, I must say. I did have something rather more romantic in mind.'

'Oh, you want romantic, do you? Well, you asked for it.'

Kate gasped as he literally swept her off her feet and swung her up into his arms. He carried her across the room, elbowed open the door, and swiftly climbed the stairs.

'Ethan. Where …?'

'I told you I wouldn't be held responsible.' His voice was rough with the intensity of his need for her as he carried her through the door into his bedroom and laid her on the bed.

'Ethan …'

But his mouth was on hers and his eager fingers were unfastening the buttons on her shirt. Kate breathed a sigh of ecstasy as his hard, powerful body moulded itself to hers and he whispered the words of love that she had waited so very long to hear.

The End

THANK YOU

Thank you for choosing this book.

I hope you have enjoyed reading it as
much as I have enjoyed writing it.

If you have, please consider leaving a short
review. Reviews make a huge difference
to an author and they really do help.

Thank you and happy reading.

ABOUT THE AUTHOR

Gail Crane

I'm lucky to live on Exmoor, one of the most beautiful places in the country, and I love reading and writing about the rich history of the area. I also write romance novels inspired by the glorious Exmoor coast and countryside.

For many years, I contributed short stories to magazines, several of which are now available as collections as ebooks and paperbacks.

I am proud to be a member of the Romantic Novelists' Association and the Alliance of Independent Authors, and in 2014 I completed a BA degree with Open University, studying creative writing.

When I'm not writing or reading, I enjoy walking and gardening and I'm addicted to coffee and crosswords.

BOOKS BY THIS AUTHOR

Flynn's Folly (An Exmoor Romance: Book 1)

When wealthy hotelier, Max Corrigan, claims part ownership of The Folly, Jessica Flynn is not about to give in without a fight. Even if he is drop-dead gorgeous.

Following the death of her father, Jessica returns to The Folly, her home on Exmoor, to find the house neglected and a once thriving business on the verge of collapse. So why has Max Corrigan invested so much money in it? And who exactly is he?

Corrigan wants his investment repaid and until then he expects a say in the running of the business but Jessica has no intention of letting a stranger take over and determines to repay the debt; and to do that she needs help. Who can she turn to? As she struggles to find a solution, she is no longer sure who she can trust, and realises she is in danger of losing everything, including her heart.

The Murder Of Anna Maria

NON FICTION

In 1858, in the isolated village of Simonsbath on Exmoor, the death of a six-year-old child by her father's hand shocked the small community.

The story of Anna Maria Burgess and the Wheal Eliza mine has since taken its place among the myths and legends of Exmoor.

The story has been told many times and, as with any story that has been told and retold as this one has been over the years, there are conflicting accounts and differences of opinion. So what really happened? What is the true version?

With the help of parish records, newspaper archives, contemporary reports of the murder and of the trial, and Ancestry.com, I have tried to piece together an accurate picture of the events that led to the deaths of Anna Maria and of William Burgess.

There are still gaps, and it is not possible to verify all reports. Newspapers then, as now, were selective with the facts and each reporter put his own spin on the story.

When a story fires the imagination as this one did, there will always be errors and inconsistencies, so it is doubtful the whole truth of the matter will ever be known; but it is my hope that this account might come close to it.

Printed in Great Britain
by Amazon

19399173R00132